W9-AWU-939

Camp Club Girls

Mystery at Discovery Lake

Renae Brumbaugh

BARBOUR
PUBLISHING

To Charis, my very own Camp Club Girl.
I love you, my sweet daughters.

"Trust in the LORD with all your heart and lean not on your
own understanding; in all your ways acknowledge him, and
he will make your paths straights."
PROVERBS 3:5–6

© 2010 by Barbour Publishing, Inc.

Edited by Jeanette Littleton.

ISBN 978-1-60260-267-0

Cover image © Thinkpen Design

Published by Barbour Publishing, Inc., P.O. Box 719, Uhrichsville, Ohio
44683, www.barbourbooks.com

*Our mission is to publish and distribute inspirational products offering
exceptional value and biblical encouragement to the masses.*

ECPA Member of the
Evangelical Christian
Publishers Association

Printed in the United States of America.

Dickinson Press Inc., Grand Rapids, MI. Job # 36502 11/13/09

Cabin 12B

"*Shhhhhh!*" Sydney told Bailey. "What was that noise?"

"What noise?" asked Bailey.

"*Shhhhhhhhhhhhhhh!*" commanded her new friend.

The two listened with all their focused energy. Then, there it was. Footsteps. Large, heavy footsteps.

The girls stood in terrified uncertainty.

Aaaaaaaaaarrrrrrrkkkkk!

Sydney gasped as the eerie shriek filled the air.

Yahahoho-ho-ho!

Bailey trembled uncontrollably as the crazy, other-worldly laugh followed.

"Run!" Sydney screamed. The two dashed as fast as their legs could carry them back toward the camp. Sydney stopped twice, waiting for Bailey's shorter legs to catch up.

• — • — •

Fourteen-year-old Elizabeth sat in the middle of the dusty road, trying to cram her undergarments back into her suitcase before anyone saw. *I thought wheels were supposed to make a suitcase easier,* she thought. Instead, the rolling blue luggage had tipped over three times before it finally popped open, leaving her belongings strewn in the street.

Suddenly, she was nearly barreled over by two girls running frantically. "Run for your life!" the smaller one cried. "It's after us!"

"Whoa, calm down." Elizabeth focused on the terrified girls.

The taller one panted. "Something's back there!"

Elizabeth looked toward the golf course but saw nothing. She noticed that the smaller girl seemed to struggle for air, and her protective instincts took over. "Calm down. You'll be okay."

"Need. . .inhaler," gasped the girl.

Elizabeth sprang into action, digging through the girl's backpack until she found a small blue inhaler. Then she helped hold it steady while the slight girl gasped in the medication. The taller girl kept looking toward the miniature golf course they'd just left. "Sorry," the small girl whispered. "I'm supposed to keep that in my pocket, but I got so excited I forgot."

"I'm Elizabeth. Why don't you tell me what happened."

"I'm Bailey," said the short, dark-haired girl. "Bailey Chang."

"And I'm Sydney Lincoln," said the tall, dark-skinned

4

girl with beaded braids. "We were at the golf course, and. . .and. . ."

"And something came after us!" exclaimed Bailey.

Elizabeth looked skeptical as she tucked a strand of long blond hair into the clip at the base of her neck.

"Is this your first year here? This is my third year here, and the most dangerous thing I've seen is a skunk."

The girls giggled but didn't look convinced. "Come with us. We'll show you." Bailey pulled Elizabeth back toward the golf course.

"I thought you were afraid of whatever it was! Why do you want to go back there?" Elizabeth asked.

The young girl stood to her full height. "Because I am going to be a professional golfer. And I'm not going to let whatever that was bully me. I plan to practice my golf strokes while I'm here."

"Will you tell me exactly what happened?" Elizabeth asked Sydney.

Sydney looked each girl in the eye and spoke slowly. "Something or someone is in the woods by the golf course. And it wasn't friendly." She paused for dramatic effect. "And. . .it came after us."

●—●—●

Kate Oliver leaned back on her bed and smiled. *Yes! I got the bed by the window!* she thought. *Hopefully, I'll be*

able to get good reception for my laptop and cell phone.
She tucked a strand of blond hair behind her ear. It was
too short to stay there and just long enough to drive her
crazy.

Bam! The cabin's outer door slammed, and Kate
heard voices. Pushing her black-framed glasses up on her
nose, she sat up. Two girls entered the room giggling and
talking.

"I can't believe I'm finally here! This is so cool. And
look at this cute little dorm room! It's just like the cabin
in *The Parent Trap*! Oh, hello!" The fun-looking brunette
with piercing blue eyes greeted Kate. "I'm Alex Howell.
Alexis, really, but nobody calls me that except my mother.
I am so excited! This will be the best two weeks ever!"

Kate smiled and reached to shake the girl's hand. "Kate
Oliver," she said. "Welcome to cabin 12B." She looked at
the other girl.

The girl's freckles matched her curly auburn hair, and she
offered a friendly smile. "Hi there. I'm McKenzie Phillips."

●—●—●

The two girls looked at Elizabeth stubbornly, as if needing
to prove their story to her. Hearing another bus pull up,
Elizabeth remembered her belongings, which were still
lying in the middle of the road.

"I'll tell you what. You help me get this awful suitcase

to cabin 12B, and then I'll walk to the golf course with you. Deal?"

Bailey's mouth dropped open, and Sydney's eyes widened.

"You're in cabin 12B?" asked Sydney.

"That's our cabin!" exclaimed Bailey.

Now it was Elizabeth's turn to be surprised. "You're kidding! Wow. It is a small world. Okay, roomies, help me hide my underwear before the entire camp sees, and we'll be on our way."

The girls gathered the strewn articles of clothing. Bailey held up one particular article of clothing and giggled. "Tinkerbell? Seriously, you have Tinkerbell on your . . ."

Elizabeth snatched the unmentionables from Bailey, crammed them in her suitcase, and snapped it shut. "Not another word, shorty!" Elizabeth scolded, but with a twinkle in her eye. The three girls chattered all the way to cabin 12B. As they approached the cabin, the two younger girls pulled their luggage out from behind some bushes.

"We sat together on the bus from the airport, and we both wanted to see the golf course before we did anything else. So we stowed our suitcases here until we got back," explained Sydney.

Elizabeth laughed. With these two as roommates, this year's camp experience would be far from dull.

The girls entered the cabin and located room B to the

right. Three girls were already there, smiling and laughing.

"Hello, I'm Elizabeth. I guess we'll be roommates!" She tossed her things on the lower bunk closest to the door, and Sydney placed her things on the bunk above that. Bailey took the top bunk next to Sydney. After an awkward pause, McKenzie stepped forward.

"I'm McKenzie Phillips," she said. "I'm thirteen, and I'm from White Sulphur Springs, Montana."

Alex bounced forward. "I'm Alexis Howell, Alex for short. I'm twelve, and I'm from Sacramento."

"Sydney. Twelve. Washington, D.C."

"Oh, that is so cool. Do you know the president?" asked Bailey, and everyone laughed. "I'm Bailey Chang. I'm nine, and I'm from Peoria, Illinois. And just so you'll all know, I plan to be the next Tiger Woods. I'll be glad to sign autographs, if you want. They'll be worth money some day."

Elizabeth stepped forward. "I'll take one, Bailey. I'll sell it and use the money for college. I'm Elizabeth Anderson, fourteen, from Amarillo, Texas."

"Well, I guess that leaves me," said Kate. "Kate Oliver, eleven, Philadelphia."

Alexis jumped up and down. "Oh, this will be so much fun! Kate brought her laptop with her. I have the coolest roommates ever!"

Everyone's attention turned to Kate's bed, which was covered with a laptop and several small gadgets. "What is all that stuff?" asked Sydney. The girls gathered around Kate's bed and watched her pull items out of a black backpack.

"It's like a magician's bag. It has no bottom," mused McKenzie.

Kate laughed. "My dad teaches robotics at Penn State, so he's always bringing home little devices to test out. Some of them are really helpful. Some of them are just fun to play with."

One by one, she pulled the oddly shaped gadgets out of her bag, describing the functions of each.

"This is my cell phone. It can take pictures and short video clips, has a GPS tracker, a satellite map, Internet access, a motion sensor, a voice recorder, and about a zillion other things!" Aiming it at the others, she said, "Say cheese!"

The other girls leaned together and smiled. "Cheeeeeeeeeeeeeese!"

Kate saved the picture then passed the phone to the others and dug through her backpack again. "This digital recorder can record conversations up to thirty feet away."

Sydney squinted her eyes. "You're kidding! That thing is the size of a contact lens! Let me see!" Kate handed her the recorder and kept digging.

"This is a reader," she continued, holding up a small penlike device.

"A what?" asked McKenzie.

"A reader. You run it across words on a page, and it records them to memory. Like a small scanner."

"That is so cool! I had no idea stuff like this existed!" McKenzie examined the reader.

"Here, I have my Bible. Will you show us how the reader works?" Elizabeth grabbed a worn Bible from her bag and handed it to Kate.

"Sure. You turn it on by pressing this button, and. . ." She ran the pen over a page in Psalms.

Elizabeth giggled. "I've heard of hiding God's Word in your heart, but never in your pen!"

The gadget girl suddenly stopped her display to announce, "Hey, I'm starved. Is anybody else hungry?"

"It's almost dinnertime," announced Elizabeth. "But first, we have some business to take care of at the golf course."

The girls listened as Sydney and Bailey described their experience.

"Whoa, cool!" exclaimed Alex. "We have a mystery on our hands! Why don't we go right now and check it out?"

"Why don't we eat first?" called out Kate. "Starving

girl here, remember?" The others laughed at the petite girl whose stomach was growling loudly.

Since it was almost dinnertime, the group decided to head to the dining hall first. Bailey led the way, taking over as tour guide.

"Wait for me," called Alex. "I need to grab my lip gloss!" She shoved strawberry Lip Smackers into her pocket.

The group wandered through the camp, with Bailey pointing out different sites. Suddenly, she stopped. "Well, guys, I hate to tell you this. . .but I have no idea how to get to the dining hall from here."

"It's this way," stated Elizabeth. "You'll get your bearings. My first year here, it took me the whole time before I could find my way around. But I get lost in a closet."

McKenzie spoke up. "Come on, girls, let's go. Remember, Kate's about to starve. We wouldn't want her to waste away to nothing."

Everyone laughed at Kate, who pretended to be nearly fainting. "I need sustenance, and I need it now!"

The group arrived at the dining hall with seven minutes to spare. They stood near the front of the line, and Elizabeth said, "Get ready for a long meal. The camp director will explain all the camp rules, introduce the counselors, and tell us more than we want to know about Camp Discovery Lake."

"Terrific." Bailey sighed. "I wanted to visit the golf course before dark."

"Don't worry," said Alex. "After the story you and Sydney told, I think we all want to find out what's down there."

"Really?" Bailey asked. "You'll all come?"

"You bet!" said McKenzie. "The girls of cabin 12B stick together!"

●—●—●

The sun was dipping behind the horizon by the time the girls left the dining hall.

"Hooray! We can finally go to the golf course!" Bailey called.

"We'd better hurry. It's getting dark," said Elizabeth.

"Yeah, and after the story you and Sydney told, I certainly don't want to be there after dark," added Kate.

The girls scurried while chattering about the different camp activities they wanted to try. Before they knew it, the sun was gone and they could barely see the road. "Why is the golf course so far away from the main camp?" asked Alex nervously.

Sydney laughed. "So nobody will get hit on the head with a stray golf ball!"

Suddenly, a voice called out from the woods.

"Who? Who? Who?"

"What was that?" whispered Bailey.

"Who?" came the voice again.

McKenzie giggled. "You city girls don't know much about the country, do you? That was an owl!"

The others burst into laughter as the voice called again, "Who?"

"I'm Sydney! Who are you?" Sydney shouted, and the laughter continued.

"It sure does get dark here, doesn't it?" said Kate. "It never gets this dark in the city."

"Are we close to the golf course?" asked Alex.

"It doesn't seem nearly as far in the daytime," Elizabeth told her.

They continued, each trying to seem brave. The trees that had seemed friendly and protecting in the daytime now loomed like angry giants. The girls' steps became slower and slower as they struggled to see where they were stepping.

Finally, Kate stopped and looked at the sky through the trees. "Look, everybody! It's the Big Dipper!" The other five girls looked to where she pointed.

"Wow, the sky is beautiful. It's so dark, and the stars are so bright," whispered Sydney.

"The stars are never this bright in Sacramento," Alex commented. "The city lights are brighter. Hey, this reminds

13

me of an episode of *Charlie's Angels,* where the Angels' car broke down in the middle of nowhere, and they had to use the stars to find their way home."

The girls were so focused on the sky that they didn't notice the image moving toward them. Kate was the first to lower her eyes, and she blinked in confusion. Adjusting her eyeglasses, she whispered, "Uh, guys?"

The girls continued pointing out the brightest stars.

Kate tried to make her voice louder, but terror kept it to a soft squeak. "G–g–guys?" The image moved closer, but still no one heard her. Finally, Kate grabbed Sydney's sleeve. "Wh–wh–what is that?" she squeaked.

Sydney looked. "Oh, my word! What in the world is that?"

The girls saw a white stripe in the road, moving slowly, steadily toward them. They were frozen, until Elizabeth yelled, "Skunk!"

Camp Discovery Lake resounded with shrieks and squeals as the girls ran back toward the cabins. McKenzie led the way with Alex close on her heels.

The girls didn't slow down until they had burst through the door of cabin 12B. Falling onto the beds, they panted then soon began giggling.

"Can you believe it? A skunk! We were scared of a little bitty skunk!" howled McKenzie.

"I don't know about you, McKenzie, but I wasn't about to smell like Pepé Le Pew out there!" retorted Alex, and the girls laughed even harder.

"Hey, Sydney, is that what scared you today? Some forest creature?"

Sydney and Bailey stopped giggling and looked at one another. "No," they replied.

"Whatever we heard was not small," said Bailey. "And it wasn't friendly."

"And it definitely came after us," added Sydney.

CHAPTER 2

Dan Ger?

"No! Make that noise go away!" Bailey groaned, pulling the covers over her head as a loud trumpet sounded reveille over the loudspeaker the next morning. "It's still dark outside!"

The wretched music continued. Apparently, the unknown trumpet player was committed to torturing the entire camp.

Sydney threw back her covers. "I'm taking a shower before all the hot water is gone," she told her roommates.

"Good idea. I'm coming, too," called Kate. Alex sat up and stretched, while Elizabeth began making her bed. McKenzie remained a motionless lump.

Alex tossed her dark curls, smiled, and began singing with an off-key voice. "It's time to get up. Get out of bed. It's time to get up, you sleepyheads!"

A pillow flew at her from Bailey's bed, but this only encouraged the perky brunette. She stood to her feet and stretched close to Bailey's ear. "It's time to get up. Get out

16

of bed. It's time to get up, you slee—"

"Okay! Okay! Promise me you will *never, ever* sing again, and I'll get up!" Bailey sat up and rubbed her eyes.

Elizabeth, spotting McKenzie's motionless form, laughed. "Alex, I think your services may be needed elsewhere."

The vivacious songbird stooped to McKenzie's level. Just as she poised her mouth to sing, McKenzie's eyes popped open. "Don't even think about it!"

They all laughed, and soon they headed toward the dining hall.

"Food at last!" Kate exclaimed as they took their places in the long line. "I feel like I haven't eaten for days!"

"You look like it, too!" announced a sneering voice. "What's the matter? Don't your parents feed you?"

The whole group turned around. "And those glasses. . . Maybe if you'd eat a carrot once in a while you could get rid of those," the very pretty, very mean-looking girl announced.

Sydney stepped forward, towering inches over the girl. "Excuse me?"

"It's okay, Sydney. I can handle this." Kate stepped forward, adjusted her glasses, and stared into the eyes of her unpleasant opponent. "It's a common misconception that small people don't eat much. However, the genealogical consequences of the high metabolic rates of both of my parents have resulted in similar metabolism in each of their offspring."

The girl stared at Kate, clearly baffled by her words. Kate triumphantly smiled.

Ever the peacemaker, Elizabeth stepped forward. "Hi! Aren't you Amberlie Crewelin? You were here last year. I'm Elizabeth, and these are my roommates, Sydney, Kate, McKenzie, Bailey, and Alex. It's nice to see you again. Oh, look! They've opened a new line. I guess we'll see you later!" Elizabeth guided the group to the other line. "We probably want to steer clear of her," she murmured to the others. "She has some. . .issues."

"Don't let her get to you," McKenzie added. "People like that are miserable, and they want to make everyone else miserable."

"Well, I don't know about the rest of you, but I'm not hungry. All I can think about is that miniature golf course and those noises we heard last night!" Bailey announced.

"Not hungry? Speak for yourself," said Kate.

Alex jumped up and down. "Let's check it out after breakfast! If we hurry, we'll have almost an hour before our first session begins. Oh! I just love a good mystery!"

"And I just love a good meal," Kate stated.

The small band of detectives moved hastily through the line and chose foods they could eat quickly. Kate loaded her plate with five fluffy biscuits and five sausage patties, drawing amused stares from her roommates. She grabbed two cartons of chocolate milk, a carton of apple juice, and a banana. She started toward the table but paused again to add an orange to her tray.

The girls settled at a table by the door and ate quickly. Kate was only half finished when the others began picking up their trays. "Hey! I'm not done yet!" she protested.

"Bring it with you," replied Elizabeth. "Here, wrap it in this napkin and stuff it in your pocket. The golf course is at the other end of the camp, so we need to hustle."

The group hurried past the chapel and around the stables on their way to the site of last night's mystery noise.

"Hello, girls!" called a man from the stables.

"Hello, Mr. Anzer," Elizabeth called back. "You all will love him," she told her friends. "He's the camp grandpa." Then, looking at her watch, she said, "We have forty-seven minutes. Last year a group was late to the first session, and the camp director made them clean the kitchen in their free time!"

"Hmm. Did they get to eat the leftovers?" Kate asked.

"*Shhhhh!*" Alex hushed them as they neared their destination. "Listen! I think I hear something!"

The young sleuths stopped in their tracks, afraid to move. Sure enough, they heard a distant howling noise.

"Is that what you heard last night?" Alex asked.

Sydney and Bailey both shook their heads. "No. What we heard was more. . ." Sydney searched for the correct word.

"Creepy!" Bailey interjected. "What we heard was like creepy laughter."

"That noise sounded pretty creepy to me," whispered McKenzie.

"Well, I don't know why we're standing here. Nancy Drew would already be investigating!" Alex exclaimed.

No one moved. "Okay. I'll go first!" said Alex. The young investigator led the way, and the other detectives reluctantly followed.

Elizabeth stopped the group as they reached the gate to the miniature golf course. "We need to stay together. We don't know what we'll find, and we're a long way from the main camp."

The girls all nodded their heads. Bailey unlatched the gate, and it swung open with a low creak. The girls moved inside and slowly approached the howling noise, which was getting louder.

"It sounds like a wounded animal," said Sydney. "Not scary, just. . .sad."

As the girls tiptoed through the golf course, they noticed the worn attractions.

"Wow! Look at this place! We don't have anything like this back in Peoria." Bailey said. "Look, there's a windmill, and a clown, and a castle. . . . It's not nearly as scary in the daylight. I'm going to come here every day to practice my Tiger Woods strokes."

Suddenly, a high-pitched, mechanical-sounding laugh came from the direction of the clown.

The girls squealed and banded together more tightly. "Or maybe I won't," continued the group's youngest member.

"What was that?" asked McKenzie. "It sounded so. . . fake."

The howling turned to a whimper, and the group froze. "That doesn't sound fake!" said Kate. Forgetting her promise to stay with her friends, she ran ahead. "Hey, get over here! Come look at this!"

The girls ran to join Kate at the windmill. They found a skinny puppy caked in mud. His paw was caught in the golf hole, and he whimpered pitifully.

Kate knelt to help the puppy. With the help of the others, he was soon free of the trap.

"Here you go, little fellow! You're okay now." Kate held the small dog close, then at arm's length. "Whoa! You stink!"

"Awww, look at him! He's hungry," said Elizabeth. "Kate, where's the rest of your breakfast?"

Kate pulled a biscuit from her pocket, and the dog

swallowed it in two bites. Then, tail wagging, he attacked his rescuer with puppy kisses, knocking her glasses askew. She offered him half of a sausage patty and another biscuit.

"Look at that. He loves you, Kate! You're his hero," said McKenzie.

"He sure ate those biscuits in a hurry. I think we should name him Biscuit!" suggested Bailey.

Biscuit wagged his tail in agreement.

Suddenly, the girls were startled by a man's voice.

"Hey! What are you girls doing? Get away from that mutt!"

An angry-looking man walked toward them. His green collared shirt showed that he was a Camp Discovery Lake staff member.

McKenzie stepped forward. "Oh, we were just looking around, and we found him. His paw was stuck in a—"

"You girls need to stay away from here. Give me that dog, and get to class!" He reached for Biscuit, but the small dog wiggled out of Kate's arms and ran toward the woods.

"But, sir, he's just a puppy! He was stuck, and hungry, and we had to help him," Elizabeth told the man.

He glared at her. "You girls aren't here to rescue dogs or to poke around an old golf course. Stay away from here, you understand?" The girls backed away a few steps.

"What are you waiting for?" he shouted. "Get out of here!"

The girls turned and ran through an open side gate, into the woods.

"And don't come back!" the angry man yelled.

They ran frantically, not stopping until they were deep in the woods. Finally, out of breath, they halted.

"Why was. . .he so angry? . . . We weren't. . .doing anything wrong," said Sydney, catching her breath.

"He seems like a. . .very unhappy. . .person to me," replied McKenzie.

Alex sank to her knees, while Bailey propped herself against a tree. Gradually, their breathing slowed, and they began to look at their surroundings.

Elizabeth leaned toward Bailey. "You okay, Bales? Got your inhaler?"

"It's in my pocket. Umm, does anybody know where we are?" asked Bailey.

"Does anybody know where Biscuit is?" asked Kate, her voice shaking.

"Biscuit! We've got to find him!" exclaimed Elizabeth. "If we don't, that horrible man will probably send him to the pound!"

The girls started yelling, "Biscuit! Come here, Biscuit!"

"Wait!" Elizabeth stopped them. "We have to stay together. The last thing we need is for one of us to get even more lost!"

"Yes, Mother," teased Bailey.

All of a sudden, a bloodcurdling scream pierced the air, followed by a rustling sound in the trees above them. The girls shrieked and huddled together.

"Wh–wh–what was that?" whispered Bailey.

"I don't know, and I d–don't want to find out!" McKenzie responded.

Elizabeth craned her neck, trying to determine the source of the alarming sound. "It sounded like a woman. A terrified woman!"

"It sounded like a cougar," said Sydney. "We studied them in my Wilderness Girls class."

"A cougar! Yikes! Let's scram!" exclaimed Alex.

"We do need to stay together," Sydney continued. "Cougars probably won't attack a group, but they sometimes attack individuals. I think we scared it."

"But Sydney, what about Biscuit?" asked Kate.

A worried silence fell over the group. Then they began calling for the lost puppy again. Just a few minutes later, they heard the rustling of dead leaves, followed by a whimper.

"Biscuit!" Kate followed the sound and pulled the bedraggled puppy from a pile of leaves. "I'm so glad you're safe!"

The girls surrounded their wiggly, smelly treasure and took turns holding him. Then the cougar screamed again in the distance.

"Let's get out of here," McKenzie urged, wide-eyed. "We may have scared that cougar, but it scared me, too!"

"You and me both," agreed Alex. "But we have a problem. I have no idea where we are or how we got here!"

The frightened young campers all looked to Elizabeth, the oldest. "Don't look at me!" she told them. "I'm directionally disabled."

"I have a compass," Kate told the group as she struggled with her wiggling bundle. They all looked at her hopefully until she added, "In my backpack. Back at the room."

"We can figure this out," asserted Sydney. "Let's think about this. The golf course is south of the main camp. We came into the woods from the right, which would be east. So, we were heading west."

"Maybe so, but we've turned around so many times, I don't remember which way is which," said McKenzie.

Five pairs of eyes remained glued to Sydney's face as she continued to work things out in her mind. She muttered under her breath, reminding herself of things she had learned in her nature studies. The others listened, not wanting to interrupt the girl who seemed to be their only hope for escape from these dark, menacing woods.

Sydney walked around trees, examining the bark, scrutinizing the branches. Her beaded braids jangled as she moved from tree to tree. Finally, she addressed her fellow campers. "To get back to the golf course, we need to head east. Look for moss growing at the base of the trees, and that will be north. Also look for spiderwebs, which are often found on the south sides of trees."

The group began to examine the details of their surroundings.

"This is fun," said Bailey. "It's sort of like a treasure hunt!"

Elizabeth stopped her search and looked thoughtful. "That reminds me of something in the Bible. Several times in Deuteronomy, God said His people are His treasured possession."

Just then, the girls heard the screaming once more in the distance. "Will you hurry up, already?" Bailey urged Sydney. The other girls tried to remain calm.

"You sure know a lot of Bible verses," McKenzie said to Elizabeth. "Let me guess. . .I'll bet your dad is a preacher!"

"Close," Elizabeth said, smiling at the insightful redhead. "My grandpa's a preacher. My dad teaches Bible at the local seminary."

"This way!" Sydney called, and the group anxiously followed her. "I see the windmill up ahead!"

Moments later, they approached the now-abandoned golf course.

"Any sign of Oscar the Grouch?" asked Bailey.

The group chuckled, and McKenzie stood on her tip toes and scanned the area. "I don't see anyone."

"Probably couldn't find a job anywhere else," muttered Sydney. "But look—someone has been digging over there, by the castle!"

The amateur sleuths walked to the fresh pile of dirt.

"It had to be the Grouch! Why would he dig here?" Alex knelt for a closer look.

"I don't know, but we'll have to figure it out another time. We'll be late for our first session," Elizabeth informed them, looking at her watch.

"What can we do with Biscuit?" asked Kate.

"If we hurry, we can take him back to the room. We'll hide him there for right now," Elizabeth told her.

As the group headed out the gate, Alex and McKenzie lagged behind.

"I have a feeling there's more to the Grouch than meets the eye," McKenzie told her friend.

The two began to follow the others until Alex spotted a small piece of paper near the pile of dirt.

"Oh my!" she exclaimed as she read it. She held it out to McKenzie.

The torn paper issued a warning: *Dan Ger.*

The girls looked at each other, then took off running, full speed ahead.

CHAPTER 3

Keep Out!

The two girls caught up with their friends in no time.

"Look what we found. By that pile of dirt," Alex panted. She passed around the wrinkled piece of paper.

Then they all spoke at once.

"What does this mean?"

"Who is this for?"

"Do you think this was meant for us?"

"I wonder if the Grouch had anything to do with this."

Sydney paced back and forth, hand to her chin. "Why do you think he was so mad at us? We weren't doing anything. That was our free time. We haven't been told to stay away from the golf course."

Elizabeth jumped in. "Speaking of free time, we may not have any if we're late. We can talk about this later. Let's go! Kate, I'll go with you to take Biscuit back to the cabin, and the rest of you get to class."

The small group of sleuths scattered.

In the cabin, Kate laid Biscuit gently on her bed. He

licked her hand, curled into a ball, and promptly went to sleep. "Poor little fellow," she said. "He's had a rough morning."

"Let's just hope he stays asleep while we're gone," said Elizabeth. She grabbed Kate by the arm and led her out the door. "I'll meet you back here as soon as this first session ends."

The two girls hurried to their classes and scooted into their seats without a moment to spare.

●—●—●

A while later, Elizabeth sat in the end chair on the back row, trying to focus on the camp counselor's words. Her mind was crowded with thoughts of puppies and cougars and cryptic warnings.

"My name is Miss Rebecca. For the next two weeks of camp, you will compete with your other five roommates as a team. Each group needs to create a team name, and whoever has the best name will receive points. You will also earn points for cleanliness, punctuality, and attitude. These points will be given at the discretion of the counselors.

"Your team will also compete in various categories in a camp-wide competition. The categories are scripture memory, nature studies, horseback riding, rowing, and a few others we'll tell you about in the next few days. On the last day of camp, the team with the most points wins the title Team Discovery Lake. Each girl on the winning team will receive a blue ribbon and a partial scholarship to next year's camp."

Elizabeth looked around at the other girls. There, on the front row, smiling sweetly at the counselor, was Amberlie.

Now that girl is trouble! Elizabeth had never gotten to know her very well, but she knew enough. All sugar and spice and everything nice around the counselors. But the minute she was away from adults, her sugar and spice turned to vinegar.

Amberlie's hand shot high into the air. "Will there be *daily* winners?" she asked.

"Good question, and yes. Each day, the team with the most points earned on the previous day will be first in all meal lines. Teams will receive daily points for attitude and for the cleanest rooms."

This announcement was followed by an enthusiastic buzz from the campers. First at mealtime—now *that* was worth competing for.

Miss Rebecca smiled as she gave the girls time to absorb the information. "Now that we've got that out of the way, let's begin our Bible Explorers class! We'll memorize a lot of scripture in the next two weeks. Let's start with a game. . . ."

Elizabeth settled back in her seat and smiled. She was good at scripture memory. This class was right up her alley.

●—●—●

McKenzie and Sydney stood with the other girls by the stable door, listening to the counselor talk about basic horsemanship. The horses all seemed gentle and trustworthy, unlike some of the stallions back at McKenzie's ranch in White Sulphur Springs.

"During your time here, you will learn basic horse care and riding techniques. These horses are used to young ladies and are calm, so you don't need to be afraid of them. However, they are very large animals, so you need to be gentle with them as well."

Sydney elbowed McKenzie. The auburn-haired girl looked at her new friend and saw her motioning to a large oak tree at the edge of the paddock. In the shade of the tree was the grouchy man from the golf course talking to the older man Elizabeth had pointed out earlier in the day. From the abrupt gestures of the grouchy man, Sydney guessed he wasn't too happy.

The girls watched and strained to hear the words, but it was no use. The men were too far away, and the counselor's words drowned out any chance of eavesdropping.

They continued to observe the exchange. The older man—Mr. Anzer—put his arm around the Grouch's shoulders, and the Grouch seemed to calm a bit. The two then walked away, continuing their conversation as they moved toward the offices at the east end of the stables.

●—●—●

Kate had signed up for the nature studies class right away. In her concrete world of Philadelphia, she didn't get much exposure to the rugged outdoors. The closest thing she had back home was the well-groomed city park or the beautiful college campus where her dad taught. She had been excited to learn about various trees and flowers and wildlife. She had even brought her cell phone so she could take pictures.

But now she could only think of the muddy black-and-white puppy asleep on her bed. *He likes me,* she thought. *I've never had a dog. I wonder if Mom and Dad would let me keep him.*

"That's about it for today, girls. As you're walking around the camp, remember to pay attention to the shapes of the leaves you see. Try to identify the ones we talked about."

Kate jerked to attention. Had she really daydreamed the whole class away? Staring at her blank phone screen, she wondered how the hour could have passed so quickly. She couldn't remember a single thing the counselor had said.

Snapping her phone closed, she remembered Elizabeth's request to meet back at the cabin. *Immediately after class.* Besides, she was eager to check on Biscuit.

Slipping the small phone into her pocket, she ran as fast as she could, nearly crashing into Bailey and Alex as she reached the crossroad that led to their cabin.

"Whoa, Kate! Slow down! At that rate, you'll have a major collision!" Alex laughed.

Kate caught her balance and smiled. "Sorry! I just can't wait to get back to the cabin. Biscuit was asleep when we left him, and I. . ." She was interrupted by a low, mournful howl.

The three girls looked at each other and exclaimed, "Biscuit!"

They ran to cabin 12B in record time. Bursting through the door, they stopped short at the sight before them.

The dirty, round-eyed puppy sat in the center of the room, tail wagging with excitement. A pair of green shorts hung off his back, and he held a dirty sock in his mouth. Undergarments, nightgowns, and T-shirts were scattered from one end of the room to the other.

"Oh, Biscuit. What have you done?" Kate scooped up the puppy, and he licked her face. "Hey, stop that!" She laughed and held him out of face range. "I don't mind the kisses, but we've gotta do something about your breath!"

"Uh, girls. . .we'd better clean up this mess. The counselors are coming before lunch to check our rooms!" said Alex.

"But first. . ." Bailey dug through her pockets. "Look

what we made for Biscuit!" She pulled out a colorful ribbon-braided rope and attached it around the dog's neck. "Alex and I worked on it in class. Now he has a collar!"

"Perfect!" exclaimed Kate. Alex and Bailey looked pleased.

"What in the...world?" The girls turned as Elizabeth stepped into the room. "Oh my." The older girl just stood, taking in every detail of the disastrous room. "Oh my, oh my."

•—•—•

Sydney and McKenzie lingered after class, pretending to admire the horses. "Do you think we should go find out what they're talking about?"

"I think we should at least see if the Grouch has an office over here or something," Sydney urged.

"That older man he was talking to, Mr. Anzer, seemed nice. Elizabeth seemed to really like him. Surely he's not like..." McKenzie paused. "No, it looked more like he was trying to calm the Grouch down, didn't it?"

The two girls walked toward the office area, pausing to look at the horses when a counselor passed.

"I want to ride the bay over there," exclaimed McKenzie.

"I think I'll stick with the pony," replied Sydney.

When the coast was clear, the girls continued to the east end of the building, pausing outside an open window.

Hearing voices inside, they grew still, straining to hear the conversation.

"I'm telling you, Dan, you can't post a KEEP OUT sign at the golf course. It may be old, but the kids still love it. You can't keep them from playing a few rounds of miniature golf if they want to."

"But William, I'm trying to get my work done. I can't make the repairs if a bunch of little girls are running around everywhere."

This was followed by a long pause.

Finally, Mr. Anzer spoke again. "Just do what you can while the girls are in their classes. I'll see if I can come help you."

"No! That won't be necessary!" Dan spoke up quickly. "I'll just figure out a way to make it work."

The two girls looked at each other, wide-eyed, but didn't move. Suddenly, the man they now knew as Dan burst through the door and nearly barreled over them. He stopped, clearly surprised to see the sleuths, and opened his mouth as if to speak.

McKenzie spoke first. "Pardon us, sir! We didn't mean to get in your way. We were just headed back to our cabin. You have a very nice day, sir! Umm. . .good-bye!"

The two girls dashed toward the cabins.

As soon as they were out of earshot, Sydney spoke up.

"Whew. That was close. I wonder if he knows we were listening."

"I don't know. I just can't figure out why he doesn't want anyone at the golf course. I mean, this is a kids' camp," McKenzie responded.

Sydney's voice rose. "Yeah. Of course kids will be running around—that's kind of the point. If it weren't for us, he wouldn't have a job here in the first place!"

"Shhhhh. We don't want the whole camp to know. Something tells me that the Grouch doesn't care much about his job. He doesn't keep the golf course tidy. He must have some other reason why he doesn't want anybody down there," McKenzie told her friend.

"I think you're right. Let's go tell the others what we heard."

The girls jogged back to the cabin, where they found the others making piles of clothing. "What in the world? What are you all doing with my shorts? And my headband? And my. . ." Sydney's bewildered gaze landed on the innocent-looking puppy sitting at Kate's feet. "Biscuit! What did you do?"

The puppy answered her with a bark and a wag of his tail.

●—●—●

The young detectives sat in a circle on the floor examining

the wrinkled piece of paper.

Dan Ger.

"Why is it written that way? You know, with a space in between, and the *D* and the *G* capitalized?" asked Bailey.

"I think the way it's written must be a clue of some sort. Maybe the space in the *middle* means we are in the middle of danger!" Sydney added.

The girls passed around the small paper, trying to find further clues. Elizabeth held the paper up to the light. "This looks like envelope paper. If you hold it up, it has a pattern, kind of like the business envelopes my parents use."

Alex reached for the paper. "May I see that?" Then, holding it up, she said, "Elizabeth is right! This may be. . . Hey! Maybe Dan is someone's name!"

McKenzie and Sydney began talking at once. "I can't believe we haven't told you yet!"

"We got so caught up in cleaning up Biscuit's mess that we forgot to tell you what happened!"

The other four sat up straight, all ears, listening to the two girls tell what they knew.

"So. . ." Alex stood, still holding the paper. "We know that the Grouch's name is Dan, so maybe this paper belongs to him. Elizabeth, can you find out Dan's last name?"

"Sure. I'll go talk to Mr. Anzer. I've been meaning to visit with him, anyway."

"Great!" Alex continued. "Kate, what else do you have in that bag of yours? Surely you have some kind of gadget to help us get to the bottom of this."

Kate sprang into action, going through her treasures and evaluating each one for its possible mystery-solving potential.

"Here's my robot spy-cam." Kate held up what looked like a remote-control four-wheeler. "We can hide and make this baby go wherever we want. The only problem is, the sound isn't that great. So we can watch what happens, but we might not be able to hear it."

"What about the tiny recorder you brought?" asked Sydney.

"I've tried that. It will work, sort of. But it's hard to get the recorder to play at the same time the video plays. So you end up watching something happen while listening to the thing that happened a minute or two before, and it gets confusing."

Elizabeth laughed. "Sort of like watching a foreign film with the words at the bottom of the screen! I can never keep up with those movies."

Alex seemed a natural fit for the role of lead detective, and the other girls listened to her instructions. "Okay, here's what we'll do. Elizabeth, you and McKenzie go back to the stables. See what more you can find about this Dan fellow.

The rest of you come with me. Kate, bring the robot."

"Sounds like a plan," said Elizabeth. "Let's go!"

Kate quickly put Biscuit into her oversize backpack and zipped it, leaving a small air hole.

Just then, Miss Rebecca poked her head around the door. "Hi, girls! I'm Miss Rebecca—oh, hi, Elizabeth! Good to see you! I'm the counselor for cabin 12. My room's at the end of the hall, in case you need anything."

"Thanks!" the girls replied, trying not to look guilty.

Miss Rebecca stood looking at the group. "Umm. . . okay then. Don't forget that now is your Discovery Time. For the next half hour, find a quiet place and study today's Bible lesson."

"Yes, ma'am," said the angelic-looking group. Biscuit whimpered, and Bailey began sneezing to cover the sound while Kate used her foot to gently push the wiggling backpack under her bed. The counselor stepped into the room and looked around with a suspicious gaze.

CHAPTER

4

Discovery Time

Bailey sneezed several more times.

"Bless you," Miss Rebecca said. She lingered a few moments, looking each camper directly in the eye. Then, with one last look around the room, she said, "Remember, I'm right at the end of the hall!" With a smile and a wave, she was gone.

"Whew! That was close!" exclaimed McKenzie as she closed the door.

Once again, Alex took charge. "Okay, you heard her! It's *discovery* time. And we have a lot of discovering to do...."

"Wait! Before we go, let's read our Discovery Scripture. That way we can talk about it while we're walking. Then we'll be doing what we're supposed to be doing," Elizabeth said as she grabbed her Bible. "Today's verse talks about wisdom. Hmm. . .let me find it. . . . Here it is! Proverbs 2:4–5 says, 'If you look for it as for silver and search for it as for hidden treasure, then you will understand the fear of the Lord and find the knowledge of God.' "

"That's perfect!" Alex exclaimed. "We are going on a treasure hunt to find clues, which will give us wisdom and knowledge about what is going on around here!"

The group laughed at Alex's enthusiasm. Elizabeth smiled at the girl as she put her Bible away. "Or something like that. . ." She chuckled. "Just remember, if any camp counselors ask what you're doing, talk about that verse."

"Okay, let's go!" The group split up, with McKenzie and Elizabeth headed toward the stables and the others toward the golf course. Biscuit poked his head out of Kate's backpack and enjoyed the ride.

As they approached the golf course for the second time that day, the girls walked cautiously and stayed in the shadows of the trees lining the road. Sure enough, Dan the Grouch was digging away.

"Why is he digging?" whispered Alex. "It looks like he's trying to find something."

"He should be trying to clean up, not making a bigger mess," added Sydney.

"Here. I brought my robot-cam. Maybe we can get a closer look," said Kate, setting down her backpack. Biscuit, glad to be free, began sniffing around the trees. The other three watched as Kate pulled out the small remote-control gadget. "I have it set to deliver the images to my phone, so we can watch from here. I'll drive, and you all can hold the phone."

"Okay, but be careful. We don't want Grouchy Dan to catch us. I've been yelled at enough for one day. He scares me," added Bailey.

The girls crouched at the edge of the golf course, hidden behind an overgrown bush. Kate held the remote, flipped the ON switch, and pressed buttons. Slowly the car moved forward.

The other girls started whispering, giving Kate directions.

"To the left!"

"No, to the right!"

"All we can see is dirt and leaves!"

"Hold it!" Kate whispered with a hint of frustration. "One person at a time, please. Sydney, you direct me."

The other girls remained quiet, and the only sound was Sydney's soft whisper, "Left. Now forward. A little to the right. . ."

Finally, she whispered, "Stop! That's perfect. We can see him. What is he looking for? He shovels, then stops and digs with his hands, then shovels some more. What does he think he's going to find?"

"Maybe he's looking for electrical wires or water pipes or something," said Kate.

"It looks like he's. . .he's. . .he's moving."

"Where did he go?" The girls didn't look up until it was too late. An angry-looking Mr. Dan glowered at them. "I thought I told you girls to stay away from here! Aren't you supposed to be somewhere right now?"

The girls sat frozen, not knowing how to respond. Finally, Bailey, remembering the Bible verse, spoke up in her sweetest voice. "We're searching for treasure, sir."

•—•—•

Elizabeth and McKenzie approached the stables, stopping to admire the horses. "That one reminds me of Sahara, my horse back home. I can't wait until I can ride the trails here," McKenzie said.

"I've always wanted horses," Elizabeth responded. "I look forward to coming here every summer just so I can ride."

"I thought everyone in Texas had horses!" said McKenzie with a laugh.

The girls continued around the stables, heading toward the office area. "This is where Sydney and I overheard the two men talking. The Grouch, or whatever his name is, seemed determined to keep people away from the golf course."

"Well, I don't know anything about him, but I know Mr. Anzer has a heart of gold. He would never let anything bad happen here at Discovery Lake," said Elizabeth.

"Did I hear my name?" Mr. Anzer asked as he walked around the corner. "Oh, hello, Elizabeth! Who is your friend?"

"Hi, Mr. Anzer!" said Elizabeth with a smile. "This is McKenzie. She's one of my roommates, and she has her own horse!"

"Is that right?" asked Mr. Anzer. "Well, feel free to hang out at the stables while you're here. We can always use an extra stable hand!"

McKenzie laughed, and Mr. Anzer motioned the two girls to join him on a long, low bench.

"Mr. Anzer"—Elizabeth looked at the gray-haired gentleman—"McKenzie and I wanted to ask you something. This morning we got in trouble by one of the staff members for being at the golf course. We didn't think we were doing anything wrong. Have the rules changed? Are we not allowed at the golf course anymore?"

Mr. Anzer looked concerned. He leaned back against the rough wooden wall. Finally, he answered, "Mr. Gerhardt is the groundskeeper for the golf course. He's a new staff member. I suppose he's just trying to figure out his job. I'm sure he didn't mean any harm."

McKenzie spoke up. "Mr. Gerhardt. . . Is his first name *Dan*, by any chance?"

"Why yes, it is," answered the old man.

Elizabeth spoke up. "Well, he seemed very upset that we were there. To tell you the truth, he was pretty scary."

"Mr. Gerhardt is a good man. He just has a lot on his mind. I'm sure he didn't mean to scare you," said Mr. Anzer.

Elizabeth and McKenzie looked at each other but said nothing. Standing up, Elizabeth told her old friend, "Thanks, Mr. Anzer. It's always great to talk to you. Maybe I'll come by for a ride this afternoon."

"That would be nice, Elizabeth. You girls go have fun. And stay out of trouble!" he said with a twinkle in his eye.

●—●—●

At the mention of the word *treasure*, Mr. Gerhardt's face went white, his eyes grew wide, and his hands balled into fists. "What do you know about a treasure? Have you found something? If so, you need to tell me about it right now!"

The girls scrambled backward.

"Tell me what you know!" the man yelled.

"Bailey was just talking about our Bible verse for today. God's wisdom is like treasure, and we have to search for it," said Kate. The other girls nodded.

Mr. Dan seemed to calm down a bit. He looked into the distance and ran his fingers through his hair. Taking a deep breath, he spoke slowly. "I didn't mean to yell at you.

But you girls need to be careful around here. You shouldn't be down here yet; free time isn't until this afternoon. You need to stay in the main part of the camp until your free time. You never know what might happen."

The girls stared at the man, not knowing what to say. He looked at them a moment longer then turned, walked to his golf cart, and drove away.

The girls collectively let out their deep breaths. "Something is definitely going on down here," said Alex.

"Yeah, that was strange. Why did he get so mad?" asked Sydney.

"He seemed almost normal until. . .until. . ." Bailey stopped. "Until I mentioned treasure!"

The other girls looked at Bailey. "Think about it," she continued. "We were hiding and spying on him. He asked us what we were doing, but he didn't freak out until I mentioned—"

"Treasure!" they exclaimed.

"That's it!" said Sydney. "He must be looking for treasure!"

"But why would he look for treasure in an old miniature golf course at a kids' camp?" asked Kate.

"That's what we're going to find out." Alex looked to be deep in thought. "I remember watching an episode of *Murder, She Wrote*, where—"

47

"Murder!" Sydney exclaimed. "Who said anything about murder?"

"Don't be silly. Nobody is going to murder anybody. Just listen to what happened in this episode, okay?" Alex continued. The girls leaned in to listen to the animated brunette describe the television mystery. "In the episode, 'Dead Man's Gold,' all of the suspects are searching for buried treasure. One of the suspects owes money to a loan shark, and he doesn't want anyone else to find the money before he does!"

"You think Mr. Gerhardt owes money to a loan shark?" asked Sydney.

"I think he's a suspect and doesn't want anyone else to find whatever treasure he's seeking," said Alex.

• — • — •

McKenzie and Elizabeth headed toward the golf course to meet the others, each absorbed in her own thoughts. Finally, Elizabeth spoke. "Well, at least now we know what the *Dan Ger* paper meant. It was just part of Mr. Gerhardt's name."

"Yeah. But, Elizabeth, I don't care what Mr. Anzer says. That man gives me the creeps!"

"Me, too. Something definitely isn't right. But I also trust Mr. Anzer. I think he'd know if we were in any danger. I guess we should just stay away from Mr. Gerhardt."

"That will be hard, since Bailey's determined to be a golf pro by the time she leaves camp!" McKenzie said. The girls laughed.

Suddenly, Biscuit loped toward them with what looked like a large metal stick in his mouth. "Biscuit!" cried Elizabeth. "Where did you come from?" She bent and retrieved a small golf club from his mouth.

"That's funny," said McKenzie. "He wants to play fetch."

Elizabeth picked up the puppy and turned her face away. "Oh, Biscuit! You seriously need a bath!" The girls continued on the path to the golf course and met the other four girls coming around the curve.

"Oh, good, you found Biscuit!" exclaimed Kate. "We thought he'd gotten away!"

"He was carrying this golf club, like he wanted to play! Isn't that funny?" McKenzie held up the club. "I'll just go put this by the fence. I'm sure Mr. Gerhardt will find it."

The four spies looked at each other, and then Sydney said, "Mr. Gerhardt?"

"Yeah, that's the Grouch's name. Dan Gerhardt."

The six sleuths exchanged information and tried to fit the clues together. They didn't notice that Biscuit had gotten ahead of them. They also didn't notice the group of girls headed right toward Biscuit.

Suddenly, their conversation was interrupted by screeches. "*Eeeeewww!* Get off of me, you filthy creature! *Help!* This dog is attacking me! Help!"

The girls ran forward, Kate in the lead, and pulled Biscuit off Amberlie Crewelin. "Sorry about that," Kate told the terrified girl.

Amberlie's fear quickly turned to disdain as she said, "Is that *your* dog? Pets aren't allowed here. I'm going to report you."

Kate dropped Biscuit. "Oh, no, he's not mine. I guess he's just a stray. Go away, little dog!" she yelled at Biscuit.

Confused, the poor dog headed toward the woods. Elizabeth spoke up. "We should go report this. Don't worry, Amberlie. We'll take care of everything. I can see you've been through enough. . .trauma."

With a snort, Amberlie gathered her group and turned. "Come on! I'll have to go back and change clothes now. That horrible creature got me all muddy."

As soon as the girls were out of sight, Kate ran toward the woods, her five roommates close behind her. "Biscuit!" they called. "Biscuit, come back!" Within moments, the puppy charged back at Kate, bounded into her arms, and gave her his slobbery greeting.

"Oh, Biscuit, can you ever forgive me?" asked Kate.

"It looks like he already has," said McKenzie.

Elizabeth looked at her watch. "Come on. We need to give this dog a bath, and if we go now, nobody will be in the showers at the cabin."

●—●—●

Sydney and Bailey peered around the cabin door to see if it was safe to exit. After a group of laughing girls wandered out of sight, they gave the signal. "Take him to the back of the cabin before you put him down," suggested Sydney.

Kate held a wet, clean Biscuit at arm's length, and the other five girls circled her to shield the dog from view. Once out of sight of the main road, Kate let Biscuit go. The dog immediately shook himself, splashing his protectors and causing them to squeal.

The puppy took their squeals as an invitation to play and began running. He ran a few yards, then stopped to see if they were chasing him. Satisfied that his playmates were following, he ran more. This continued as the girls tried to catch the damp puppy without drawing attention to themselves.

They finally cornered the dog, dried him, and combed his hair. Then they stood back to admire the handsome dog before them. No one would ever recognize him as the muddy stray they had found that morning.

Biscuit took their looks of approval to mean that they wanted to play some more, and with a bark and a wag of his tail, he was off. The girls kept him cornered, but no one could catch him.

Finally, Kate disappeared into the cabin and returned with a handful of cheese crackers. "Here, Biscuit! Here, boy! I don't have a biscuit, but trust me—you'll love these!"

Instantly, the dog bounded to her, and she knelt to feed him. "That's a good boy! Now, we have to leave you behind while we go to our next classes. If you're good, we'll have more food for you!"

The girls once again hovered close together to hide their new pet from view. They placed him inside the room and closed the door. Almost immediately, the howling started.

"Shhhhhhh! Make him stop!" Alex whispered. "I think I see Miss Rebecca coming up the road!"

Elizabeth opened the door, and the howling stopped. She closed it, and the noise started again. She and Kate slipped inside.

"What are we going to do?" whispered Kate. "We can't leave him here! We'll have the whole camp investigating our cabin!"

"I know," said Elizabeth. "We'll just have to take turns taking him with us. I know you're pretty attached to him, and he fits perfectly in your backpack, so you take him with you now."

"Uh, I don't think that will work," responded Kate.

"Why not?" asked Elizabeth, surprised.

"Because my next class is a cooking class. He will never stay still and quiet if he smells food!"

"Hmm. . .you're right about that. I'm going on a nature walk, so I guess I'll take him with me. I think Bailey is in that class, too. We'll stay at the back of the line. Here, let me borrow your backpack."

Outside, the girls greeted their counselor, chatting to cover their nervousness.

"Hi, Miss Rebecca! How are you?"

"Do you like being a counselor here?"

"We're so glad you're in our cabin. You're the coolest counselor."

The pretty young woman laughed and again eyed the group with gentle suspicion. "What are you girls up to? Don't you need to get to your next classes?"

Then she noticed that they were all water splashed. "What in the world have you been doing? Swimming isn't until this afternoon! And, ew! What is that smell?"

The girls exchanged panicked looks. Would Miss Rebecca figure out their secret?

Moans, Howls, and Growls

The girls stood in silent guilt, wondering how to respond.

Miss Rebecca laughed. "I'll tell you what, girls. I don't even want to know what you've been up to. But I want you all to march right back into your rooms and get some clean clothes on. Come with me."

Sydney began speaking loudly, hoping that Elizabeth and Kate, still inside the room, would hear. "Yes, Miss Rebecca! We'll go inside this very minute to change our clothes! We are coming inside right now!"

The girls stood in front of their door, none of them wanting to open it while Miss Rebecca was with them. The counselor, with an expression of confused amusement, stepped forward and opened the door herself.

As the door groaned open, Kate and Elizabeth stood there innocently, ready to head out the door. "Oh, hello everyone! We were just leaving. See you all later!" Elizabeth called as she and Kate left the room. The counselor just shook her head and continued down the hall. The girls all sighed in relief that she didn't notice what the rest of them saw clearly. The backpack draped over Elizabeth's shoulders was *moving*.

The four girls quickly changed their clothes and hurried to their next classes.

The next few days passed in a whirlwind of camping activity and Biscuit training. Before long, the young dog knew how to sit, stay, fetch, and roll over. The girls learned that as long as he wasn't left alone, he wouldn't howl. But keeping him with someone at all times was becoming more and more difficult.

"I have an idea," said Bailey one evening as the girls prepared for bed. "I've visited the golf course several times a day to practice, and I haven't seen Mr. Gerhardt there since that first day. But every time I go, I see new places where someone has been digging. He must dig at night. . . . Anyway, why don't we leave Biscuit at the golf course during the day? It's far enough away from the camp that if he howls no one will think anything of it."

"That's a great idea, Bailey!" said Elizabeth, combing out her blond tresses. "That would sure make things easier. I don't know about the rest of you, but I've had some pretty close calls with the little guy."

"Me, too!" said the other five girls.

"Hmm. . ." Alex fluffed her pillow and crawled under

her covers. "I wonder why the Grouch has disappeared during the day. And why in the world would he dig at night?"

"I don't know, and I don't care," said Bailey. "I kind of like having the golf course to myself. I stay away from him, he stays away from me, and everything's good."

The girls turned the light out and stopped talking, until Bailey broke the silence. "But then, there are still those noises."

Sydney sat up, flipped on the lamp by her bed, and asked, "Noises?"

Bailey covered her eyes with the pillow and said, "Turn that thing off!"

"Bailey, what noises?" McKenzie asked.

Bailey rubbed her eyes. "Well, there's that weird laughing thing that happened on the first day. And sometimes I hear moans and howls and a deep, low growly thing."

The other girls were wide-awake. "Bailey, what are you talking about? Why on earth would you keep going down there?" Elizabeth asked her.

"Well, the first couple of times it happened, it scared me. Good thing I had my inhaler with me! But I finally figured out that it must just be the golf course. Those noises are wired up somehow—probably to make the course more interesting. They don't even bother me anymore."

Alex dangled her feet from her bunk and asked, "Do you hear the noises every time?"

"No," Bailey answered. "A couple of times I've been there and nothing has happened. But I think the digging must have tripped a wire or something."

"Why do you say that?" asked Kate.

"Because every time I go near a hole, I hear one of those freaky noises. As long as I stay clear of the holes, everything stays quiet."

The girls thought about that for a moment, and then Alex piped up. "I remember an episode of *Scooby-Doo* where—"

The other five moaned, and Kate threw her pillow at the pretty brunette. "Not again, Alex! You and your Hollywood mystery solving. . ."

"Seriously, you guys! Listen to me! In one episode. . . actually, in several episodes, there were these spooky noises! They almost always turn out to be someone hiding and making the noises go off when the characters are close to solving the mystery! The noises are a fear tactic. Whoever is causing them doesn't want Bailey near those holes!"

The room grew silent as each girl digested Alex's information. Once again, Bailey broke the silence. "Well, that's just great. I was getting used to the noises. Now I'm going to have to use my inhaler again."

"You could just stay away from the golf course," Elizabeth told her.

"Are you kidding? I have to practice my strokes! You'll be glad, too, when I'm rich and famous. You'll be able to say, 'I knew her when. . .' "

The girls laughed, and Sydney turned off the lamp. "We'd better get some sleep," she said. "We'll talk about this more in the morning."

●—●—●

Early the next morning, before the trumpet wake-up call, Alex sat up in bed. "I have a great idea!" she called to her roommates.

The girls groaned and moaned, but Alex didn't let that stop her. She hopped out of bed and continued chattering. "We can attach Kate's tiny recorder to Biscuit's collar, and we'll leave him at the golf course. Then, we can hear the noises Bailey told us about. If they go on and off all day, we'll know they're just random. But if they only sound when people are there, we'll know someone is making them go off."

"Yes, but what if it's Bailey making them go off? What if she's just accidentally stepping on something?" asked Sydney.

"We'll figure that out later. First, let's just find out if

they happen all the time or just when people are around," Alex told her.

"Uh, guys, you're forgetting one thing." Everyone looked at Kate, who was still in bed. Her muffled voice came from under the covers. "If we leave Biscuit alone at the golf course, he will howl all day. That's all we will hear."

Alex sighed. "You're right. I didn't think about that."

The conversation was interrupted by the wretched trumpet music, and the rest of the girls began crawling from their beds. When the song ended, Elizabeth spoke. "We could try it anyway. Maybe we'll hear something in the background, even over Biscuit's howling. It can't hurt to try."

Hearing his name, the puppy poked his head from beneath the covers at Kate's feet and barked.

"Come on, boy. I'll take you outside." Elizabeth scooped up the small dog and tucked him into the folds of her robe. She carried him outside, behind the small cabin, and waited for him to do his business. Biscuit had just disappeared behind some trees when she was startled by a voice behind her.

"Elizabeth, what are you doing out here?" Mr. Anzer called from the road. He was making his morning golf-cart drive through the camp.

"Oh! Mr. Anzer, you startled me! I was, uh,. . .I was

just out enjoying the sunrise!" Elizabeth smiled at her old friend.

Mr. Anzer gave her a puzzled look. "Elizabeth, how many years have you come to this camp?"

"This is my third year, sir."

"Then you should know that the sun rises in the east. You are facing west."

Elizabeth giggled nervously. "Oh, I guess that's why I missed it. I never was very good with directions."

Mr. Anzer shook his head, waved good-bye, and drove away. The girl breathed a sigh of relief and scooped up the puppy, who was now at her feet. "Biscuit, you are a lot of trouble, you know that?" she scolded the dog, then kissed him on his cold, wet nose. "But I suppose you're worth it."

●—●—●

The girls hurried to the old golf course before breakfast. When they arrived there, Kate knelt to check Biscuit's collar. "The recorder is attached securely, and. . .there. I turned it on. So now, we'll just wait and see what happens." She gave the little dog one last hug, placed him inside the gate, and closed the latch.

Sydney and Alex jogged around the course to make sure no other gates were open. When they were convinced that all was secure, they called good-bye to the little dog, who had retrieved a golf club and sat expectantly wagging his tail. When the girls turned to walk away, his tail sank. He dropped the golf club, gazed after them with sad eyes, and began howling.

"Just keep walking," said Elizabeth as Kate and Bailey paused. "Going back will just make it harder."

"This is breaking my heart," said McKenzie, trying not to turn around. Somehow, they ignored the dog's soulful cries and kept walking to the dining hall.

As the six roommates stepped into line, they were rudely pushed aside by Amberlie and her crew. "Pardon me, excuse me, step aside, please," said Amberlie in a commanding voice. "Make way for the Princess Pack. We won the clean cabin award yesterday, so we go first. Move out of the way."

Elizabeth stifled a laugh, Bailey let out an exasperated moan, and Sydney tried to keep from rolling her eyes. "Oh, my, my," said Sydney. "The *Princess Pack*? We cannot, and I repeat, *cannot* let Amberlie win this competition. What are those counselors thinking, awarding her more points than the rest of us?"

"Don't worry, we can catch up," Elizabeth told her friends. "So far, the only real points awarded are for clean cabins. Let's just make sure ours is really clean today. But first we need to come up with a team name."

"I've been thinking about that," said Bailey. "I think it should have something to do with the fact that we're at camp."

"Let's make it a name to reveal that we are members of an elite group," said Alex.

"How about the Discovery Lake Discoverers?" suggested McKenzie. "No, it's too much of a tongue twister."

"I think we should keep it simple," said Elizabeth. "Something easy for everyone to remember."

"So. . .we want to have a camp club, or something like that," said Kate.

"I've got it!" said Bailey. "We can be the Camp Club Girls!"

"I like it! It's simple and to the point," said Sydney.

"Very well, then. We are the Camp Club Girls!" said Elizabeth, and the group let out a cheer.

•—•—•

After breakfast, the Camp Club Girls hurried back to their cabin and cleaned it to a high shine. "I love Biscuit, but he sure is messy! It's a lot easier to clean without him dragging everybody's socks out!" said McKenzie.

"Tell me about it! He thinks my panda is an intruder! Every time I take it off my bed to make it up, he attacks it!" said Bailey.

"We need to decide who will compete in which camp

event," Elizabeth told them. "McKenzie is the natural choice for horseback riding. We'll also need a team for the canoe races and someone to compete in the nature studies quiz. And, of course, the talent competition."

The girls talked at once, discussing who wanted to do what.

"Kate, why don't you do the nature studies quiz, and I'll do the scripture memory competition," Elizabeth suggested as she helped Bailey straighten the covers on her bed.

"I think this competition is in the bag!" exclaimed Bailey, heaving her giant panda back onto her bed.

"I do think we have a good chance, but it will be tough. Amberlie seems pretty competitive. She really wants to win," McKenzie told her friends.

"She can want it all she wants," said Sydney, "but we want it more. And we're gonna win!"

●—●—●

Kate left her nature studies class, pressing past campers returning to their cabins. When she was halfway to the golf course, Elizabeth caught up with her.

"I'll bet I know where you're headed," said the fourteen-year-old.

Kate sighed. "I feel guilty about leaving Biscuit alone. But I know it's best this way. I've just never had a pet before. I wish I could talk Mom and Dad into letting me keep Biscuit."

Elizabeth smiled. " 'Delight yourself in the Lord and he will give you the desires of your heart,' Psalm 37:4. That's today's Discovery verse. I guess you could say that a dog is one of the desires of your heart."

"Yes, it is. I guess I'll have to think more about that verse. Maybe there is hope, after all," Kate responded. "Come on, let's go. I miss Biscuit!"

They jogged the rest of the way to the golf course. As they approached, they heard the low, mournful howls that told them two things: Biscuit was safe, and Biscuit was very, very sad.

The little dog lunged at Kate, nearly knocking her to the ground as soon as she slipped inside the gate. "Biscuit!" she exclaimed. "I've missed you, too, boy! I'm sad when we're apart!"

The dog attacked her with slobbery kisses and muddy paws.

"Hey! Stop that!" Kate laughed at the dog's enthusiasm.

Elizabeth smiled at the girl and dog who were so in love with each other. "Boy, that bath didn't last very long," she said. "Now be still, Biscuit, and let us listen to your collar."

•—•—•

Alex and Bailey returned from their crafts class, each

holding a small wooden treasure box. Bailey's sparkled with glitter and plastic jewels, while Alex's was painted with bold stripes. Arriving at their room, they stopped. They stared. Then the girls jumped up and down, cheering.

A cardboard trophy with the glittered words CLEAN DORM WINNER—25 POINTS hung on their door.

"We won!" The two girls squealed.

That is how Kate and Elizabeth found their two friends moments later. They had run all the way from the golf course, and now they were panting. "Girls, listen. . ."

Kate stopped and fell onto her bed, trying to catch her breath. Holding up the small recorder, she said, "Listen."

They were interrupted by Sydney and McKenzie, who had seen the trophy on their way in the door.

"Hey, cool! We won! Now, unless Amberlie can rack up some serious character points, we'll be first in line all day tomorrow," said McKenzie with a grin.

"I can't wait to see Amberlie's face when we pass her," Sydney said.

"Well, don't act too smug. The Princess Pack is still way ahead of us in overall points. Remember, they've won three days in a row! We still have some serious catching up to do," said Elizabeth.

Kate, now recuperated from her run, waved her arms. "Guys," she called out. "I think this is more important than standing first in line. Listen to what was on Biscuit's recorder!"

The girls gathered around Kate's bed and leaned in to hear the tiny device.

"Sounds like howling, just like you said," McKenzie told her.

"Shhhh! Just listen."

The girls strained to hear something, anything, over Biscuit's desperate howling. Then, after about thirty seconds, the howling stopped.

Digging for Treasure

The girls looked at each other and continued listening. In the background, they heard what sounded like the low rumble of a truck's engine. Then the engine died. They heard a door slam and heavy footsteps approach.

The footsteps ended with what sounded like a cell phone ringing then a man's voice. "Hello? Oh, hi, Dad. Yeah, I've been digging. No, I haven't found anything. No, no sign of any treasure. But I'm not giving up. Don't worry, I'll find it. I'll call you as soon as I know something."

The talking ended, and then the footsteps started again. Only this time, they seemed to be going away from the recorder. A car door slammed, an engine revved, and then it seemed the truck drove away. When the noise from the vehicle faded, Biscuit started howling again.

The girls sat in silence.

Finally, Alex spoke up. "Well, girls, the plot thickens."

"I'll say," said Bailey. "I guess that explains all the holes."

"So, Mr. Gerhardt *is* digging for treasure. . . ." McKenzie looked thoughtful. "I wonder what his dad has to do with all of this."

"Yeah," said Sydney. "And if his dad is in on it, does he come here and help his son?"

Elizabeth just sat quietly, soaking it all in. Finally, she spoke up. "Well, we have a full-blown mystery on our hands. And it's up to us to get to the bottom of it. But for now, let's only go to the golf course in groups of two or more. No more going down there alone, okay Bales?"

"No problem! I almost needed my inhaler just listening to the recording!"

•—•—•

Elizabeth dangled her feet over the side of the dock and watched the ripples from the rock she had just thrown. Her Bible was open on the dock beside her, and her eyes focused on the verse she had read three or four times. She read it out loud, as she often did when trying to memorize something:

"Matthew 6:19–20. 'Do not store up for yourselves treasures on earth, where moth and rust destroy, and where thieves break in and steal. But store up for yourselves treasures in heaven, where moth and rust do not destroy, and where thieves do not break in and steal.' "

Lord, there sure is a lot of talk about treasure here at

camp this year. I want to have the right kind of treasure—the kind that will make You happy. But what about the mystery at the golf course? Is a treasure really buried there or somewhere around the camp?

When she heard the soft murmur of a golf cart drawing near, she knew it was Mr. Anzer. He faithfully made the rounds in that golf cart, watching over the camp, making sure everything was running smoothly. She smiled at the man who reminded her so much of her grandpa.

"Hello, Elizabeth. I had a feeling I'd find you here in your old spot. Don't let me disturb you. I'm just going to check the pedals on these paddleboats. They've been sticking. I'll bet they just need some oil." The old man pulled an oil can from the toolbox in the back of the cart.

"Oh, you're not disturbing me. I was just thinking about this morning's verse. I've noticed all of our verses so far have talked about treasure, and I think it's funny."

"Funny?" Mr. Anzer's eyebrows lifted.

"Oh, not funny, ha-ha. The other kind of funny."

The old man began examining the pedals of a boat banked along the edge of the lake. "Tell me why it's funny," he said.

Elizabeth leaned back and looked at the sunlight glistening through the branches. She didn't want to reveal

69

too much of the mystery, but she did want some answers. Something told her that Mr. Anzer was a good source of information.

"Oh, my roommates and I have just been playing sort of a. . .a mystery game. We're pretending a treasure is buried somewhere in the camp. It's silly, really. But we're having fun."

The old man stood and looked at her. "Well that is funny. Just where do you think this treasure may be hidden?"

Elizabeth laughed nervously. "Oh, it could be any-where—the stables, the nature trail. . .the golf course. . ."

Mr. Anzer turned his attention back to the pedals. "I've been working here for a long time, and I've never run across any buried treasure. But that doesn't mean it's not here!" The man chuckled. "If anybody can find treasure in this old camp, I'm sure it will be you."

Elizabeth smiled. "How long have you worked here, Mr. Anzer?"

"Oh, longer than you've been alive. Years ago, I was the manager of camp operations. All three of my children attended this camp every summer, and my wife used to oversee the cafeteria. She died a few years back, and my kids are all grown and married. I just can't bring myself to leave this old place. . . ." He paused and smiled. "So now, I just putter around and fix things."

"It sounds like a fun job to me," Elizabeth told him, and he smiled at her. "I have a question, though. This is such a great camp, and everything is kept in top shape—except for the golf course. It seems kind of run-down, and that doesn't fit in with the rest of the camp. Why?"

Mr. Anzer moved to the next paddleboat and knelt to check the pedals. "The golf course was a main attraction when the camp was new. But years ago, it turned out that a gang of thieves had their hideout on the old Wilson farm—just on the other side of the golf course. When they were discovered, we increased the security here at the camp. For a couple of years, we didn't let any campers go down that way—the golf course was off-limits. Then, even when we reopened it, most of the campers were a little spooked by the idea that thieves might have hidden there. It just never became a popular attraction again. And with a tight budget, maintaining the golf course never seems to become a priority."

"Wow, that is kind of scary. Any chance the gang is still there?" Elizabeth asked.

"No. This happened a long time ago. I don't know what happened to the thieves, but I'm sure they wouldn't come back to the same place where they got caught," he told her.

Elizabeth picked up her Bible and stood. "I need to do

something before my next class, Mr. Anzer. It's been really nice talking to you."

The old man waved good-bye and continued on to the next paddleboat. "See ya later," he called.

Elizabeth hurried toward the cabins. *Wait till the others hear about this!* she thought. *This is more complicated than we thought.*

A few minutes later, she flung open the door to find her roommates getting ready to leave for their next classes. "You will never believe what I just found out!" Elizabeth announced.

●—●—●

That afternoon, the girls used their free time to explore the golf course. They greeted a very excited, muddy Biscuit, and slipped through a small opening in the far side of the fence.

"The old farmhouse has to be this way," said Sydney. The six young detectives, with their four-legged sidekick, tromped through thick trees and brush until they arrived at a clearing. There, just beyond a trickling creek, was an old farmhouse.

"This is it!" said Alex. "This is just like in *Dragnet!* I watch those reruns all the time with my grandpa. Once they were looking for—"

"Shhhh!" whispered the other girls in unison.

"We don't know what we'll find," said Elizabeth in a hushed voice. "Whatever happens, let's stay together."

The girls nodded, gingerly walked through the shallow creek, and approached the old house that was falling apart. The only sounds were the gentle rustle of trees swaying in the breeze and Biscuit's steady panting.

They noiselessly drew closer to the old farmhouse until they were close enough to peek through a broken window. Old newspapers and discarded fast-food containers littered the floor, and tattered furniture was flipped this way and that in careless disarray.

A Biscuit began to growl, and the girls froze. The dog's growl grew louder, until finally he dashed toward the trees. Standing on his hind legs, he looked ready to scale the tree.

A squirrel chattered angrily from its branches. The girls sighed with relief and continued exploring.

Alex motioned for the group to follow her. "This way," she whispered, and the band of detectives stepped carefully around the corner of the house, onto the steps of the wide porch, and through the door, which hung only partially on its hinges.

"Wow, this looks like something out of a scary movie," said Bailey.

The girls spread out through the small downstairs area,

turning chairs upright and peering in closets.

"Whoa! Bad move!" they heard Sydney call from the kitchen. She had opened the refrigerator, and the foul stench spread through the rest of the house in moments.

"Ugh! Gross!" The other girls covered their noses. Kate and McKenzie pulled their T-shirts up over their faces, leaving only their eyes visible.

Elizabeth rushed to open a window, but she found it painted shut. Then, spying a back door in a corner of the kitchen, she opened it wide. "At least there's a breeze. Maybe it will blow the smell away." Sure enough, the odor began to die down.

Alex stood at the foot of the stairs, looking into the shadowy hallway above. "Hey, let's go upstairs and look around."

The girls looked at each another, waiting for someone else to go first.

"Uh, you go on ahead, Alex," said Sydney.

"Awww, come on, guys. You're not scared, are you?" she prodded them.

"I'm not scared. Are you scared?" Sydney retorted.

"No, I'm not scared," Alex shot back. She remained glued to her spot.

Finally, Kate led the way. "Okay, Alex. Come with me."

Then she said, "If we're not back in ten minutes, run for your lives!"

The other girls laughed nervously then followed Alex and Kate up the stairs. "We might as well stick together," said Elizabeth, bringing up the rear. Biscuit bounded up the stairs ahead of them and rushed into a dark room.

The girls followed their beloved mascot into a dusty bedroom. McKenzie pulled back the curtains and lifted the shades, and sunlight flooded into the room. Biscuit sniffed here and there and then dove under the bed. A moment later, he reappeared with an old sock in his mouth.

"What is it with you and socks, boy?" asked Kate, kneeling to scratch him behind the ears. The girls opened drawers and closets, finding a moth-eaten coat, a muddy pair of brown work boots, and more old newspapers. The small connected bathroom revealed a rusty drain, a dried-up cake of soap, and a roll of yellowed toilet paper.

Together, the girls moved to the next bedroom, and this time Elizabeth opened the curtains. As the other girls snooped around, Elizabeth stood at the window. She noticed a ladder propped up against one side of the window. Then her gaze went to the driveway leading to the farmhouse. The mud showed fresh tire tracks, but she saw no vehicles. Funny, she hadn't noticed those earlier.

The house certainly looked like no one had been inside for a very long time, so why the tire tracks?

She turned from the window, not wanting to frighten the younger girls. "I think we should head back," she told the others. *I'll tell them about the tire tracks after we're safely back at camp,* she thought.

"Hey, look at this!" said Kate, pulling a faded spiral notebook from a drawer in the bedside table. "It looks like an old journal of some sort. But it must have gotten wet, because most of the words are washed out."

The girls crowded around, looking at the cryptic notebook. Biscuit, still carrying the old sock, hopped onto the bed beside Kate and made himself comfortable.

Bang! The girls jumped at the noise from downstairs. Their eyes filled with panic as they heard heavy footsteps. Bailey opened her mouth to scream, but McKenzie clasped her hand over Bailey's mouth. The girls remained frozen as the footsteps got louder. Quietly, Elizabeth tiptoed to the door, shut it softly, and turned the lock. Then she looked at the girls, held a shushing finger over her lips, and tiptoed to the window.

No one moved except Elizabeth, who skillfully opened the window. In a soft whisper, Elizabeth said, "We need to stay calm. Here's a ladder, but we have to be extra quiet, or whoever is downstairs will catch us. Sydney, you go first and help the others down. I'll stay here and go last."

Sydney's eyes widened, but she tiptoed to the window, slipped over the ledge, and scurried down the ladder. Bailey went next, then Kate, holding the notebook. After that, McKenzie descended with Biscuit. Alex grabbed an old newspaper before heading down. Finally, with one last look around, Elizabeth started out the window.

Just after Elizabeth's feet hit the ground, the ladder tipped. Before the girls could catch it—*crash!*—it landed on the ground.

"Hey!" a man's voice yelled.

"Run!" shouted Elizabeth. The girls took off. Through the creek they splashed, as heavy footsteps followed.

Just when it seemed they would escape, Bailey tripped over a large root. The others stopped to help her, but Elizabeth shouted, "Go, go, go!" She helped Bailey to her feet.

The girl gasped for air. Elizabeth felt in her friend's pockets until she located the inhaler. She looked around but saw no one. She stood with Bailey, holding the inhaler in place and coaxing her friend to breathe slowly.

Finally, Bailey pushed the inhaler away. "I'm okay," she said. "Come on, let's get out of here."

The girls jogged after the others. As they reached the fence line for the golf course, Elizabeth stepped into the shadows of a large tree, turned, and looked.

Missing Jewels!

Elizabeth caught up with the other girls. They lingered by the golf course gate, making sure Bailey was okay, all talking at once and trying to make sense of what had just happened.

Biscuit stood patiently with a golf club in his mouth until Kate finally threw it. He immediately retrieved the club and begged her with soulful eyes to throw it again. The other girls chattered on with frightened, excited exclamations.

"Did you get a look at him?"

"No, but he sounded big!"

"How do you know it was a man?"

"Well, the footsteps sounded big. I don't think a woman would walk that loudly."

"Well, I think it was the Grouch," said Bailey.

Finally, Elizabeth spoke. "I saw him."

Everyone looked at her. "Bailey is right. It was Mr. Gerhardt."

"I knew that man was trouble! He is definitely up to no good," exclaimed Alex.

"I don't know," Elizabeth mused. "He walked back toward the farmhouse, but he didn't look angry or scary. His shoulders were down, and he just looked. . .I don't know. I thought he looked sad."

"Well, I think you have too much compassion. He nearly scared us to death, remember?" Sydney reminded her.

"Yes, but perhaps he didn't mean to scare us. He couldn't have known we were there. Maybe we scared him!" Elizabeth countered.

The other girls stared at Elizabeth as if she'd lost her mind. Finally, McKenzie spoke. "Let's get back to the cabin. I need some time to relax. I think I'll change into my swimsuit and head down to the pool."

"Now that sounds like a great idea!" Alex agreed. The group said good-bye to their puppy and headed back toward the main camp.

•—•—•

That evening, Sydney and Alex wandered to the front of the dinner line, where Elizabeth was holding their place. They smiled in response to congratulations and good-natured "Just wait until tomorrow! We'll win!" from other campers.

They were almost to the front when Amberlie blocked their path. "Enjoy your short-lived victory, girls," she sneered. "Tomorrow, you all are toast!"

The two girls scooted around their ill-tempered rival and greeted Elizabeth at the front of the line.

"What was that about?" Elizabeth asked.

"Oh, nothing. Just Amberlie being herself," said Sydney.

When the girls had their food and sat down, talk quickly turned to business. "We have to get to the bottom of this mystery," said Alex. "Elizabeth, I know you think Mr. Gerhardt is some poor, sweet man, but I think he's looking for something. I think he's one of the thieves!"

"I didn't say he is poor or sweet! I just think there is more to him than meets the eye," said Elizabeth.

"I agree with Elizabeth," McKenzie announced. "And I agree with Alex. Mr. Gerhardt definitely has something to do with this mystery, but we need to find out more facts before we accuse him of anything."

The conversation halted as a shadow fell over the table. The girls looked up to find—of all people—Mr. Gerhardt. He stood at the end of their table, looking at Bailey, not saying a word.

They all remained still, waiting for him to say something. Bailey squirmed.

Finally, the man spoke. "Are you enjoying camp?" he asked.

They nodded.

"That's nice," he said. Then he turned and walked away.

No one spoke for a moment.

"What in the world was that about?" Sydney asked.

"That man gives me the creeps," said Bailey.

"My point exactly," said Alex, picking up where the conversation left off. "Let's hurry and go back to the room. Kate, can you do an Internet search?"

Kate, mouth full, looked longingly at her heaping plate. She swallowed, then answered. "I'll do anything you ask. Just don't rush me!"

Later that evening, Elizabeth leaned over Kate's shoulder, watching her type various phrases into the search engine. "Try 'thieves near Camp Discovery Lake,'" she suggested.

Kate typed in the phrase. The words "Sorry, but there are no results for that term" appeared on the screen.

Kate breathed a frustrated sigh. "The problem is that all of this took place before everyone had access to the Internet. So, unless someone has written about it on the Web, we won't find anything."

Bailey and McKenzie lay on the floor, flipping through

the water-stained notebook Kate had found. "This is useless, too. The ink is too faded to read," complained McKenzie.

Alex and Sydney had divided the old newspaper, and each scanned through the stories. "This newspaper is over twenty years old. It's crumbling in my hands," said Sydney.

"Surely we'll find some kind of clue here. Let's keep looking," Alex encouraged the group. She gently turned the pages, reading headlines.

"Wait, I think I found something!" exclaimed Sydney. "Look! It's only one paragraph, but it says that a jewel thief has been convicted. And, oh my goodness. You are not gonna believe this. . . ." Sydney continued to stare at the page.

"What? Tell us!" the girls urged her on.

"The name of the man who was convicted. . ." Sydney looked at her roommates.

"Come on, spill it!" Alex nearly shouted.

"William Gerhardt!"

"I knew it, I knew it, I knew it!" exclaimed Bailey. "I knew that the Grouch was no good!"

"There's more," continued Sydney. "It says the jewels were never found."

"Maybe the thief was Gerhardt's father!" said Alex. "And now Dan is trying to recover the jewels!"

Kate began typing on her computer again.

"Jackpot!" she cried, and the girls gathered around her. "The search for 'William Gerhardt, jewel thief,' turned up six, seven, eight different articles! Looks like we may solve the mystery, after all!"

"And look what I just found," said McKenzie. "It's hard to read, but it looks to me like an address. And right above, it says, 'Manchester Jewels.' Is that the name of the jewelry store that was robbed?"

Kate clicked on an article and lifted her arms in victory. "Mystery solved. It says right here—William Gerhardt was convicted of grand theft for robbing Manchester Jewels, a large jewelry store in Springfield. That's about an hour from here."

They all chattered at once, celebrating this new information. Then Kate lifted her hand. "Not so fast. It says here that the jewels were never found. He was convicted by a jury with a seven-to-five vote. Nearly half of the jurors didn't think he was guilty."

"Of course he was guilty. Why else would his son be digging for the jewels? He must know they were hidden somewhere at the golf course," said Sydney.

The girls sat in puzzled silence. Finally, Alex spoke. "Kate, you come with me. We need to go get Biscuit. And we have a little more discovering to do."

"I'll come, too," said Elizabeth.

"Not me," said Bailey. "I'll save my trips to the golf course for the broad daylight!"

Sydney and McKenzie, tired from a long day, decided to stay with Bailey.

●—●—●

The three girls approached the golf course, using Kate's cell phone as a flashlight.

"Shhhh! Listen," Kate whispered just before they rounded the curve leading to the gate.

"What is it?" asked Alex.

Kate motioned for them to scoot into the woods behind a thick crop of trees. "Biscuit is either gone or he's not alone. He's not howling."

"You're right," whispered Elizabeth.

"Well, we can't just stand here. I'll tell you what. . .I'll go on around through the gate, and you two stay here in case something happens," suggested Alex.

"No, I don't like that idea. We need to stay together," said Elizabeth.

"Shhhh! What's that?" Kate interrupted.

The girls quieted, straining to pinpoint the sound. "It sounds like digging," said Elizabeth. "Let's sneak to the fence and see what we find. Kate, snap your cell phone shut, or whoever that is will see us for sure."

Kate closed the phone, and the only light left was the soft moonlight. Slowly, the girls crept through the brush until they arrived at the fence line. A twig snapped beneath Elizabeth's feet, and the girls froze. Then a soft whimpering moved toward them. "Biscuit!" whispered Kate, and the little dog lunged at her face, kissing her with wet, sloppy kisses. She stifled a giggle, and the other two girls shushed her.

"Be quiet! I think I see someone," Alex whispered. Sure enough, the girls could just make out the figure of a man. The digging had stopped, and the man stood still, looking their way.

"Who's there?" he called.

The girls crouched in the shadows, holding their breath and praying Biscuit didn't make any sudden moves. The dog wiggled in Kate's arms, but his preoccupation with kissing her kept him from making much noise.

"Hello?" the figure called again. Suddenly, a bright flashlight snapped on. The girls remained still as statues, praying the man wouldn't see them. Slowly, the beam passed through the woods to their left, traveled in front of them, then continued to the right.

Finally, after many long moments, the light was snapped off, and eventually the digging resumed. Still, the girls remained, partly because they were too frightened to move, and partly because they wanted a better look at the man's face. They thought they knew who it was. They just wanted to be sure.

A cloud passed in front of the moon, leaving them in complete darkness. Then the cloud moved away and rays of moonbeams fell directly on the man's face.

Mr. Gerhardt was digging.

Noiselessly, the girls tiptoed back through the brush to the road. As soon as they were out of sight of the golf course, Kate snapped her cell phone back on, casting a soft blue glow around their path. They remained silent all the way back to the cabin.

An hour later, the girls were still awake, talking about the mystery.

"Well, we know Mr. Gerhardt is guilty. We just have to prove it," said Sydney.

"I'm not sure I agree," said Elizabeth. "Sure, he's looking for the jewels. Sure, he has some kind of interest in this case. But I keep thinking about that Internet article Kate found. Surely, there must have been some reason why the jury was so divided."

"I'll research more tomorrow," said Kate. "But I'm tired of thinking about it. Biscuit and I want to go to sleep." She pulled the covers over her head then started giggling. "Biscuit, stop it! Biscuit, quit licking my toes! Stop!"

Before long, the whole group was laughing at Kate and the small dog.

"Well, I do have one more thing I want to talk about before we go to sleep," said Bailey. "Who wants to be in the talent show?"

The giggles turned to groans, and Bailey sat up. "Come on, you guys. We need those points!"

"I think you should do it, Bales. You have Hollywood written all over you," said Alex.

Bailey's face lit up with a smile. "Well, okay, if you insist! I was in the spring talent show back home in Peoria, and I can do my singing and dancing act. I did happen to bring the music and props with me in case they had talent shows here. But I need someone to play the piano for me," she said.

No response.

"I need someone to play the piano for me," she repeated.

Silence.

"Elizabeth, don't you play the piano?" Bailey continued.

Elizabeth leaned up on her elbows. "I don't like to play in front of people."

"Awww, come on, Beth! Pleeeeeeeaaase? Pretty please with a cherry on top? For me?" Bailey begged.

More silence.

Finally, Elizabeth sighed. "Okay."

"Hooray! Oh, thank you, thank you, thank you! You're the greatest! I know we'll win. We have to start practicing tomorrow. Isn't there a piano in the dining hall? I wonder if they'll let us use that. How about during our free time? Or maybe sooner. Maybe we should wake up early and go practice. I have this great tap dance I do, and the song is so fun. It goes like—"

"Go to sleep, Bailey!" chimed five voices in unison.

● — ● — ●

Early the next morning, Bailey and Elizabeth walked to the dining hall. The sun was barely peeking over the trees, and Bailey was humming and singing her song so Elizabeth could learn it.

It goes like this, Beth:

I love being beautiful,
Being beautiful is grand,
With my hair just so, and my eyes all aglow,
A new dress, and my nail-polished hands!

"I have some pink spongy rollers for my hair and some of my mom's face cream! Won't that be hilarious? I'll be out there, my face all creamed up, rollers in my hair, tap-dancing and singing about being beautiful!" Bailey's excitement grew as they entered the dining hall.

Elizabeth laughed at Bailey's enthusiasm. "You will be the star of the show," she told her. "Now, where is the music?"

Bailey pulled the sheet music out of her backpack and handed it to Elizabeth.

Sitting down at the old piano stationed to one side of the stage, Elizabeth began flipping through the pages, becoming familiar with the chords and the key changes. "This music has several key changes. I'm not sure I can play it like it's written; I'd need to practice this for weeks. But the chords are listed, so in some parts I'll just play those. I'll jazz it up here and there. I think it will be fine."

Bailey smiled. "I know you can do it!" she encouraged.

Elizabeth began playing with Bailey singing along. After a few rough starts, she finally sang through the piece.

"Okay, now let's try it with me on stage. We'll go all the way through without stopping," Bailey instructed. Elizabeth began to play, and Bailey began singing and dancing her heart out. She performed to the empty room as if it were an audience of hundreds. At the close, she held out her last note, arms high in the air, and then finished with a grand curtsy.

Both girls were surprised when applause came from a corner of the room. Amberlie stepped out of the shadows.

"Very nice, for an amateur. Your little act will add

some good variety to the show. But you certainly won't win the grand prize. Your talent doesn't even come close to mine. Sorry to break it to you, kiddo, but you don't have a chance."

Bailey's smile turned into a frown as she responded, "How dare you! You are so. . ."

"Amberlie! We didn't know anyone was here. So great to see you. Did you want to practice? Here, we were just finishing. Come on, Bales. Let's go." Elizabeth gathered the music, grabbed Bailey by the arm, and walked past Amberlie.

When they were outside, Bailey let loose. "How could you just let her talk to us like that? She is so mean! I'd like to give her a piece of my mind!"

"Bailey, that's exactly what she wanted us to do. If we act like her, she wins. She knows she got to us. Sometimes it's best just to play dumb," Elizabeth said.

"Play dumb?" Bailey questioned.

"Pretend you don't know she's being mean. And keep being nice. Then she looks bad, and you look like a saint. Eventually, she'll go away and be mean to someone else," Elizabeth explained.

"But then she wins!" complained Bailey.

Elizabeth laughed. "That's where you're wrong. Right

now, she's back there trying to figure out why she didn't intimidate us. We won."

As they rounded the corner leading to the cabins, they nearly collided with Sydney, who was running at full speed. "Elizabeth! Bailey! Come quick!"

CHAPTER
8

Into the Darkness

The girls rushed back to their cabin, where Alex and McKenzie leaned over Kate's shoulder, reading something on the Internet. "Unbelievable," Kate was saying.

"But that doesn't mean anything. I still say he's guilty," Alex responded.

"I don't know. I just don't know," said McKenzie.

Elizabeth jumped in. "Would somebody please tell us what is going on?"

"Yeah," added Bailey. "What's so unbelievable?"

Kate looked over her shoulder and said, "Listen. 'William Gerhardt was convicted of grand felony theft and sentenced to twenty-five years in prison,' " she read aloud. " 'The conviction came beneath a shroud of doubt and questionable evidence, with a seven-to-five jury convicting him. Gerhardt, an employee of Manchester Jewels, is accused of selling the jewels on the black market. The jewels have not been found. In a post-trial interview, jurors continue to debate the legitimacy of the evidence presented.' "

The girls listened eagerly.

"If he sold them, why is Mr. Gerhardt looking for them?" asked Elizabeth.

"Well, I still say Gerhardt is guilty. I mean, look at his son, the Grouch. That man is digging, breaking into abandoned houses, chasing little girls... That's not exactly normal, innocent behavior," said Sydney.

"Perhaps we should wait until we know more before we make up our minds," Elizabeth told her friends.

"I agree with you," said Alex as she smoothed on her strawberry lip gloss. "As a matter of fact, I think we should do a little more investigating of our own as soon as possible."

"Well, I think we should eat," said Kate. "It's time for breakfast, and if we don't hurry, they'll start without us. That would be a waste of a perfectly good front-of-the-line pass."

"You're right," said Bailey. "Is the room ready for inspection? I'd love to win again today."

"Yep," said Sydney. We delivered Biscuit to the golf course and made sure everything was perfect before we started the Internet search."

"Hello! Starving girl here, remember?" called Kate. "You all stay here and gab all morning if you want. I'm leaving!"

The other girls laughed, and then they followed their

tiny, hungry roommate to the dining hall.

• — • — •

During breakfast, Alex brought up the mystery again. "Nancy Drew always says, 'Drastic times call for drastic measures.' I think we need to snoop around Mr. Gerhardt's office."

Elizabeth held her fork in midair, deep in thought. "When did Nancy Drew say that?" she asked.

Alex giggled. "Well, come to think of it, I'm not sure she did say it. But somebody said it, and I agree."

"Okay, Miss Hollywood. What do you think we should do? Just waltz into Mr. Gerhardt's office and snoop through file cabinets and desk drawers?" asked Bailey.

Alex smiled. "Yes, that's exactly what I'm suggesting. And I think I may have the perfect plan. . . ."

The girls leaned together and began making plans, when suddenly Amberlie fell in front of their table, sending scrambled eggs, orange juice, and dishes in every direction. The girl began crying in a loud, dramatic voice, "They tripped me! Those mean girls tripped me!" She pointed at the Camp Club Girls.

The girls were caught off guard, and when a counselor rushed over to help Amberlie, she looked at the six roommates with a disappointed expression. "Is this true?" she asked.

"Yes, it's true. I saw it," said one of Amberlie's sidekicks.

"I saw it, too," testified another of Amberlie's friends.

"I'm not sure which girl it was, but I definitely saw a leg stick out just as Amberlie walked by," said one of the girls.

"Yes, and just before that, they were all whispering together, like they were planning something," said the other girl.

"I saw that, too," said the counselor. She turned to the six roommates and asked, "Which one of you tripped Amberlie?"

The girls just looked at her in stunned silence.

"Okay then, if none of you will tell the truth, I'll have to punish all of you." Then, zoning in on Elizabeth, she said, "I'm disappointed in you. You know we don't put up with that kind of behavior here."

Elizabeth found her voice. "But we didn't trip her! We were talking about something totally different!"

The counselor looked at her. "Then tell me what you were talking about."

The six girls looked at each other. They certainly couldn't tell her they were planning to sneak into Mr. Gerhardt's office and snoop.

Their silence sent the wrong message. "That's what I thought," said the counselor. "All six of you will be on clean-up duty for two days. You can start right now."

The girls began gathering their trays as Amberlie and her two buddies stood looking innocent. As the counselor walked away, Amberlie gave the group a smug grin.

Sleuthing would have to wait. It looked as if the girls would spend every free moment of their next two days in the dining hall.

●—●—●

After lunch on the second day of their punishment, Elizabeth scrubbed burned goo from the bottom of a pot with furious determination. Her roommates worked around her, talking, laughing, and flicking soapsuds on each other. But Elizabeth worked in silence.

She was too angry to speak.

I don't understand, Lord, she prayed silently. *We didn't do anything, and Amberlie is so awful. Didn't you say You would not let the guilty go unpunished? So why are we scrubbing pots and mopping floors, when the guilty one is probably out riding horses and having fun right now? It's not fair. We should be enjoying our camp experience. Instead, we are stuck here.*

Bailey interrupted her thoughts. "Elizabeth? Did you hear me?"

Elizabeth jerked to attention. "I'm sorry. Were you talking to me?" she asked.

The other girls laughed. "That pot doesn't have a chance against you," McKenzie said. "You're attacking it like it is your worst enemy."

Elizabeth smiled, but inside she still felt mad. She knew she had to forgive Amberlie. But she wasn't quite ready to do that.

"They want to hear our song, Beth. I was asking if you'd play for me. C'mon. We need the practice, and it'll be fun. We are allowed to take breaks, you know." Bailey spoke with a pleading voice. "Pleeeeeeeeeeeeeeaase?" she begged.

Elizabeth nodded, set down the pot, and wiped her hands on a dish towel. She walked to the piano and sat down.

Bailey scrambled to get the sheet music out of her backpack then placed it on the music stand. She described her crazy costume to the girls then nodded at Elizabeth to begin.

Before the song was halfway through, each member of the four-person audience was on the floor in fits of giggles. "That's the funniest thing I've ever seen!" laughed Alex. "I think you two should go to Hollywood for an audition!"

Sydney held her side; she was laughing so hard she couldn't speak. Tears streamed down Kate's cheeks, and McKenzie let out a giggling sound that sounded partially like a monkey and partially like a chicken. The silliness of it all, paired with the girls' tiredness, made everything funnier. Before long, Elizabeth and Bailey had joined the laughter.

This was how Miss Rebecca found them. She silently stood in the doorway, and one by one, the Camp Club Girls noticed her. Slowly, the laughter died as the girls waited to see what their counselor had to say.

An amused smile spread across the young woman's face. "Carry on," she told them, then turned and walked away.

After a few moments of stunned silence, the silliness continued. After all, Miss Rebecca had told them to carry on. Who were they to disobey a camp counselor?

●—●—●

After dinner that night, the girls moved slowly, mopping, sweeping, and scrubbing dishes. Bailey stifled a yawn and brushed a wisp of hair out of her eyes. "I am going to sleep well tonight," she said.

"I still can't believe we've been stuck working here for two days," said McKenzie. Then she chuckled. "It has been kind of fun, though."

"Yeah, sort of like in those *Facts of Life* reruns, when Jo, Blaire, Tootie, and Natalie had to paint the dorms," said Alex. "Or when they had to work in the cafeteria serving line."

"Oh, I remember seeing that show. Yeah, I guess we are kind of like those girls," said Sydney.

Once again, Elizabeth remained quiet. Yes, she'd enjoyed some fun moments during the two days of clean-up duty. But she was still angry at Amberlie. She would need a little more time to get over this injustice.

The room fell into a comfortable silence as the tired girls finished their final duties. Suddenly, they heard voices from the office next to the dining hall. They didn't think much of it—counselors came and went from the office all the time. They had a special area there where they could relax away from the campers.

Then the name "Gerhardt" caught their attention. They looked at each other then strained to hear the words.

"Such a shame, really. It has taken over his entire life," said a high-pitched voice.

"How much longer until he gets out of prison?" asked a lower female voice.

"I don't know. He must be getting close to the end of his time. But Dan is still obsessed with finding new evidence."

"Do you think his dad is really innocent?" asked the lower voice.

"Who knows. But it's sad. Dan talks to his father every chance he gets. And Tiffany said he gets a letter almost every week postmarked from the prison. She delivers them to his office, and he keeps them all in a desk drawer, tied with brown string."

"What if his dad is guilty, and Dan's trying to. . ."

"Don't even say it. I've said too much as it is."

With that, the distant conversation turned to which flavors of ice cream were stored in the lounge freezer.

—•—•—

Back at the cabin, the girls practically fell into bed. "I don't think I've ever been this tired!" groaned Bailey.

"Me neither. But now I won't be able to sleep. We've got to get our hands on those letters!" said Alex.

"I'm starving." Kate sighed. "All that work has really built my appetite."

Elizabeth reached under her bed. "Well, I have just the cure. I've saved these for an emergency. After all we've been through, I'd say we've earned them." She pulled out three boxes of Ding Dongs, and the girls suddenly found new energy as they pounced on her bed.

"You've been holding out on us!" chided Kate. "I'm surprised Biscuit didn't find these."

Elizabeth laughed and passed out the treats. "I had them zipped inside two plastic baggies, then locked inside my suitcase."

Kate sat up suddenly. "Biscuit! We were so tired we forgot him! We can't leave him there all night!"

"Kate, don't you think he'll be okay? I love the little guy, but I'm sooooo tired!" said Bailey.

Kate reached for her flashlight and stood. "It's okay. I'll get him."

"Oh, no you don't," said Elizabeth and Alex together.

"You can't go out there alone at night. I'll go with you," said Elizabeth.

"And this is the perfect time to snoop around Gerhardt's office. I'm coming, too," said Alex. "Kate, grab that reader-pen-thingie of yours, the one you showed us on the first day of camp."

The other girls looked at Alex as if she'd lost her mind. "Are you kidding?" asked Sydney.

"No, I'm not. We're going down there anyway, so why not make the most of it? It's dark, so no one will see us," Alex persuaded. "If Gerhardt shows up, well. . .we'll just cross that bridge when we come to it."

The other girls stared at her. Finally, Kate dug through her backpack. "She's right. We might as well kill two birds with one stone," Kate told them.

Elizabeth spoke up. "We don't all need to go. That will just increase our chances of getting caught. Sydney, McKenzie, and Bai—" Stopping, she looked at Bailey's bed. "Look. She's out like a light."

Elizabeth continued. "Sydney and McKenzie, you stay

here. My cell phone is in my suitcase, and we'll take Kate's cell phone. If we get into trouble, we'll call."

The girls looked at each other with fear and excitement. Finally, McKenzie spoke. "Be careful."

With a wave, the three girls stepped through the door and into the darkness.

●—●—●

The howling got louder the closer they got to the golf course. "Well, at least we know he's okay," said Alex.

"Poor little guy. We've really neglected him the last couple of days," said Kate around a mouthful of Ding Dong. "Remind me to bring him an extra sausage in the morning."

The little dog pounced on them as they entered the gate. Kate scooped him into her arms. "We're so sorry, boy. We'll make it up to you, we promise."

Suddenly, Biscuit jumped out of her arms and bounded into the darkness. He returned a moment later carrying a golf club in his mouth, and the girls laughed.

"He likes to play fetch more than any dog I've ever known," said Elizabeth.

"Well, we'd better get down to business and get out of here. Let's see if Mr. Gerhardt's office is unlocked," said Alex, drawing them back into detective mode.

Kate shined the light of her cell phone, and the girls

tiptoed to the small building that housed the golf clubs, balls, and a small office for the groundskeeper. Rattling the door, they discovered it was locked.

"Let's try the window," Alex suggested. They moved to the side of the building. Biscuit stayed close to their feet, sniffing the area protectively.

The window was small and high off the ground. Elizabeth, the tallest, pushed on the window pane, and it easily opened.

"You're the smallest," Alex told Kate. "We'll push you through, and you can look around."

"Okay, but you guys are gonna owe me big-time for this," Kate said. Then, looking straight at Elizabeth, she said, "I'll take my payment in Ding Dongs."

The two taller girls hefted Kate through the window. She landed on the floor with a loud thud. "I'm okay," she reassured.

"What do you see?" asked Alex.

"Nothing," Kate replied. "You still have my light."

"Oh, sorry," called Elizabeth, standing on her tiptoes. "Here, I'll drop it down." She held the phone through the window and released it.

"Owwww!" came Kate's voice. "Right on my head!"

"Sorry!" Elizabeth called out.

They heard Kate moving inside. "Okay, here is the

desk. Now, I just have to—"

Her voice was cut off by the sound of a truck's motor. Elizabeth and Alex ducked behind a bush just before two headlights flashed onto the building. The motor died. A door opened and closed. The girls heard footsteps and then keys jangling. They heard a click, a door opening, and then the window lit up as the person inside switched on the light.

"Prince"

Kate had just removed the stack of letters from the desk drawer when she heard the truck's motor then saw a flash of headlights through the window. Thinking quickly, she noticed a small closet in the corner of the room. Clutching the letters, she moved around a couple of large storage boxes, slipped into the closet, and shut the door. Her cell phone light revealed a large pair of men's boots with a long overcoat hanging above them. A couple of dirty shovels rested in the opposite corner. She stepped into the boots and slid her body into the middle of the coat, hoping to disguise herself in case someone opened the closet door.

She tried to quiet her breathing and wished she could soften the pounding of her heart. She heard the click of the office door opening, then saw light beneath the crack in the closet door. Heavy footsteps were accompanied by whistling. . .was that a praise song?

The footsteps came toward the closet, and the door

creaked open. Kate held her breath and prayed like she had never prayed before. *Please, Jesus, don't let me die. I'm too young to die.*

Large hands reached into the closet, grabbed the shovels, then shut the door. She then heard rustling outside the door and assumed the person was searching through the boxes. She heard a scooting sound, and the light from the crack in the door was covered. After more rustling, the footsteps retreated. The light clicked off and she heard the outer door close. Slowly, quietly, she let herself breathe.

Thank You, God; thank You, God; thank You, God, she prayed. Then she reached for the door handle and pushed. The door wouldn't budge. Apparently, one of the boxes had been moved in front of the closet door. She was stuck!

Kate took a deep breath and told herself not to panic. She slid to the floor and pulled out the letters. If she was going to be stuck in a dark closet, she might as well make the most of it.

●—●—●

Elizabeth reached for Alex's hand in the dark. Biscuit nuzzled between the two girls, and Alex scooped him up. Neither girl made a sound as they peered through the small shrub. They watched the truck park. The headlights died. They heard the truck door open, then footsteps, accompanied by whistling. Elizabeth recognized the tune—the campers had sung it that afternoon at the worship service.

The girls heard a door opening. Suddenly, light flooded out of the window above them, and Alex gasped. Elizabeth held a finger to her lips. The girls remained still as opossums, staring at each other and squeezing hands.

After what seemed an eternity, the light disappeared, the office door opened and closed again, and the footsteps retreated. The two girls sat, afraid to move. Finally, Alex whispered, "What do you think happened to Kate?"

"I don't know. I guess she found a place to hide," Elizabeth spoke softly. Then she stood to her toes and strained toward the window. "Kate!" she whispered urgently.

No answer.

"Kate! Answer me!" Elizabeth urged.

Still no answer.

The clouds shifted, casting moonlight on the area. Elizabeth looked at Alex and said, "I'm going in. Help me up."

"What? You can't leave me out here alone!" whispered Alex.

"I have to. We have to find out if Kate is okay!" Elizabeth answered.

"Well, let's both go," Alex whispered back.

"We can't both get in. Besides, one of us needs to stay here in case something happens," Elizabeth said firmly. "Now help me up. Please."

"Okay," said Alex. "But this is not going like I thought it would." She clasped her hands and held them down so Elizabeth could use them as a step.

Struggling, Elizabeth wiggled through the window, landing with a thud on the other side. She stood, rubbed her sore backside, and groped through the dark.

"Kate!" she called desperately.

"Elizabeth! Is that you?" Kate's muffled voice came through the darkness.

Elizabeth stumbled around the room, feeling the wall, trying to find her friend. "Kate, where are you?" she called.

"I'm in the closet. Something is in front of the door!" she called out.

Elizabeth felt around until she located the boxes and the door. It took all of her strength to push aside the large box, but soon the closet door was free. Kate stepped out, and the light of her cell phone cast a soft glow around the room. The girls peeked in the box to see hammers, wrenches, and a pile of oddly shaped metal tools. The girls breathed deep sighs of relief.

"What ha—"

"I was so sca—"

Both girls started whispering at once, and this started them in a series of nervous giggles.

"I can't believe this is happening. Did you get the letters?" Elizabeth asked.

"Yes, but we need to put them back and get out of here. I used my reader pen and recorded about a dozen pages, but it was dark, and I had a hard time seeing the lines. We may end up with a bunch of gibberish, but hopefully we'll have something we can use," Kate told her.

The girls jumped when they heard a voice through the window. "Hey! Are you two okay?" Alex frantically whispered.

"Yes, we're fine. We'll be right out," Elizabeth told her.

Elizabeth turned to Kate, "We'd better go out the window so no one knows we've been here."

Kate hurried to the desk and replaced the letters. They scooted the desk chair beneath the window and climbed back through the opening. Each of them stifled cries of pain as they landed on the scratchy branches of the small shrub.

"Finally!" Alex exclaimed. "I was starting to think you were going to have a slumber party in there!"

In the excitement, they hadn't heard the sound of footsteps drawing closer. Suddenly, a flash of light shined through the window. "Hey! Is somebody in here?" Mr. Gerhardt demanded from inside the office.

The girls paused. Then, without saying a word, they ran full speed through the darkness. Alex still clung to Biscuit, and they were just rounding the corner when they heard, "Hey! You girls! Come back here!"

The girls ran faster than any of them had ever run in their lives. They were too afraid of what might happen if they stopped!

Finally, they arrived back at cabin 12B. Sydney and McKenzie sat on the front steps in their pajamas.

"Oh, thank goodness you're back! We were just trying to decide if we should come after you!" whispered McKenzie. The five girls entered the cabin, three of them holding their sides from the pain of the long sprint. The clock read 12:33 a.m. when the whispers stopped and the girls finally slept.

• — • — •

During Discovery Time the next morning, all six girls dangled their feet from the dock. They had elected Elizabeth to lead them in their devotions, and now they listened to her read the scripture from her Bible.

"Proverbs 10:2, 'Ill-gotten treasures are of no value, but righteousness delivers from death,' " she read.

"I definitely agree with the first part!" said Kate.

"Why?" asked Elizabeth.

"I guess you could call those letters last night, 'ill-gotten treasures.' We could have been arrested for breaking and entering! We had no business going through Mr. Gerhardt's letters, and now they have no value."

The girls nodded. They had been disappointed that the reader pen hadn't delivered more information. The closet had been too dark for Kate to run the pen evenly along the lines. Most of the lines were scrambled, and what little they could read was just about prison life.

"Well, we may not have acted in 'righteousness,' but it sure felt like we got delivered from death!" exclaimed Alex.

"Oh, I know it! I was so scared! I just knew we were going to. . ." Kate was interrupted by loud squeals from Bailey.

"Eeew! Gross! Get that thing away from me!" she yelled. The other girls laughed when they saw the source of panic. It was a tiny green lizard that had climbed onto the dock and almost into Bailey's lap.

"Awww, look at him! He's cute," said McKenzie. She scooped up the lizard and held him for the others to see.

"Step back, Mac!" squealed Bailey to McKenzie.

Alex, Elizabeth, Sydney, and Kate crowded near McKenzie for a better look, while Bailey kept her distance.

"I wish we could keep him," sighed Kate.

"No!" said all five roommates. But Elizabeth took the lizard from McKenzie and studied it.

"We can't keep him. But maybe we should hang on to him for a few hours. I have an idea. . . ," she said with a mischievous grin.

●—●—●

McKenzie helped Sydney into the saddle of a gentle-looking mare. "This will be fun," she told her friend. "This will be the first time I've gotten to ride the trails since camp started."

Sydney looked at her freckle-faced friend. "He seems pretty gentle. I've always wanted to ride a horse."

McKenzie chuckled. "She. The horse is a she. Her name is Sugar. I've helped Mr. Anzer a few times with the grooming, and she's a sweetie. You'll like her." She then adjusted the saddle on a strong black quarter horse, stepped into the stirrup, and pulled herself into place. "This is Spirit. He's well trained and full of energy. He reminds me of Sahara, my horse back home."

The two girls were about to hit the trails when Mr. Anzer and Mr. Gerhardt rounded the corner and approached them. The girls avoided Gerhardt's eyes and focused on Mr. Anzer.

"Hello, girls," Mr. Anzer said. "Headed out?"

"Yes, sir," they responded.

"That's nice. It's a lovely day for a ride," he said with a smile. Then, his expression changed to one of concern. "Say, girls, Mr. Gerhardt told me that some campers were fooling around at the golf course late last night. He said he thought it might have been some cabin 12 girls, though he didn't get a good look. Were you at the golf course after dark last night?" He looked straight at McKenzie then at Sydney.

The two girls looked at each other then back at Mr. Anzer. "No, sir," they answered.

He eyed them steadily, then said, "That's good to know. You two be careful, and have fun!" The smile returned to his face, and he waved as they rode through the gate and toward the trails.

"That was close," said McKenzie as they got out of earshot. "I wouldn't have lied to him."

"Me neither," said Sydney. "My mom says withholding information can be like lying, though."

The girls grew quiet, enjoying the beauty of the trails. Suddenly, they heard giggling from the trees. Out of nowhere, a fat water balloon exploded on the trail in front of them, spooking Spirit and causing the horse to whinny, rear back, then take off in a full-speed run. Red hair streamed in the wind as the horse rounded the curve and sped out of sight.

Sydney turned to see Amberlie and her friends running away. She decided she would deal with them later. Right now she had to help her friend.

● ━ ● ━ ●

McKenzie clutched the reins. After a brief scare, she realized the horse was staying to the trails. Eventually, they would circle back to the stables. She held her head back, enjoyed the wind on her face, and let the horse run. After a few minutes of a thrilling ride, she felt the horse getting winded. Tugging gently on his reins, she guided him to slow down.

"I don't know where that balloon came from, Spirit! I'm sorry it scared you," she told the horse, rubbing him gently behind the ears. "Sydney will be worried. We'd better go find her."

She gently guided the horse to turn around and head in the opposite direction. Before long, she met Sydney, who was coaxing Sugar into a slow, labored gallop. McKenzie had to chuckle at the sight of her friend bravely coming after her on the slow horse. "I'm okay," she announced.

"Well, that's good," said Sydney. "I didn't know whether to come after you or to go back and get help. Either way, Sugar doesn't know the meaning of 'Hurry up'!"

McKenzie guided Spirit to turn around once again, and the girls continued down the trail. "Did you see who threw the balloon?" McKenzie asked.

"Do you even have to ask?" Sydney responded.

McKenzie nodded. "It's a good thing Spirit is well trained. That could have been really dangerous."

"I don't understand that girl. She's so fake around the counselors. But she's the meanest girl I've ever seen. I almost feel sorry for her," said Sydney.

"Yeah, I'd love to know what's going on inside that head of hers. She obviously has some problems." McKenzie looked thoughtful.

The two girls settled into a comfortable silence; then Sydney started laughing.

"What's so funny?" McKenzie asked.

"Elizabeth's plan. Never in a million years would I have thought Elizabeth was capable of coming up with something so. . .so. . ." Sydney searched for the word.

"Naughty?" McKenzie helped her out.

The girls chuckled and talked about the plan for the rest of the trail ride.

●—●—●

The campers had just been released from the evening meeting, and groups of girls were ambling toward the cabins. No one was ever in a hurry to get ready for bed.

Amberlie and her roommates were about to turn down the path leading to cabin 8 when Bailey and Alex stopped them. "Amberlie, could I talk with you for a minute?" Alex asked sweetly.

Amberlie looked at the two with a mix of curiosity and suspicion. "What do you want?" she asked. Amberlie's roommates stood by, listening.

"I was just wondering if you are a cheerleader," asked Alex.

Amberlie was taken off guard. "A what?" she asked.

"A cheerleader. Are you a cheerleader at your school?"

Amberlie paused. "No," she said.

"Oh, that's a shame. You've got the perfect build to be a cheerleader. And you're so pretty. You should think about trying out," Alex told her.

"Uh, okay," Amberlie responded. She clearly wasn't sure how to take the compliment.

"If you'd like, I can show you some moves. Here, watch this," Alex continued, then demonstrated a double forward handspring. "It's really not as hard as it looks," she continued.

During this conversation, Elizabeth, Sydney, Kate, and McKenzie watched from behind the trees at the side of the road. When Alex had Amberlie's full attention, the four

Camp Club Girls, along with the lizard, sneaked toward cabin 8.

"Shhhhh!" Elizabeth told her giggling friends, but she had a hard time controlling her own giggles. She removed a small jar with holes poked in the lid from her tote bag. "You all stay here and keep watch. I'll go in and put Prince under Amberlie's covers. She always brings a pillowcase with her name on it, so I shouldn't have any problem finding her bed."

"Okay, but hurry!" McKenzie told her. "I'm not sure how long Alex can keep them entertained!"

Elizabeth surprised them by standing tall and walking right into cabin 8 as if she had every right to be there. It took her only a moment to locate the pink ribboned pillowcase with the name AMBERLIE embroidered across the top. Carefully, she turned back the covers, then gently removed the small lizard and kissed him on the head. "Do your job, Prince," she said. She tucked the creature under the blankets and smoothed them back into place.

The other three girls stood in the road, trying to act casual. A few moments later, Elizabeth darted out of the building then slowed down. The four girls walked toward their own cabin, trying to control the laughter that bubbled up inside them.

Alex and Bailey caught up with them at their cabin door, and the girls circled toward cabin 8 again. They hid in the bushes outside the windows of Amberlie's cabin. This would be a show they didn't want to miss.

Missing Biscuit

The Camp Club Girls could hear the conversation from Amberlie's room drifting through the open window.

"We're going to beat those girls from cabin 12. And it's going to start tomorrow night at the talent show. After that, we'll win the horse-riding match and the canoe races, no problem," said Amberlie.

"What about the scripture memory competition? That Elizabeth is good. She's won all the practice competitions in class," said a voice Elizabeth couldn't place.

Amberlie laughed. "Yes, but she hasn't been up against me yet. My dad's a preacher, and I've memorized scripture since before I could walk. No way she'll beat me."

The girls looked at one another. "A preacher's kid? Amberlie's dad is a. . ." Bailey felt Elizabeth's hand cover her mouth.

"Shhhhh!" The other girl whispered. The light went out in cabin 8, leaving only the soft glow of a lamp. Slowly, the Camp Club Girls peeked in the window, just in time to see Amberlie pull back her covers.

The girl was wearing pink satin pajamas, and her head was covered in pink hair curlers. She slid leisurely beneath the covers and reached for the lamp. She clicked it off, and all went black. Not a sound.

The six girls outside the window waited for several minutes then looked at each other in the moonlight. Disappointed, they turned to go back to their cabin. They had just stepped into the shadows of the trees when they heard the loudest, shrillest, most chilling scream.

"Help! Help me! Heeeeelp! Get it off, get it off, get it off! Eeeeek! It's in my hair! Get it off! Ew, ew, ew! Heeeeelp!"

The cabin door flew open, and Amberlie dashed outside, jumping up and down and smacking herself in the head, yanking out her curlers and screaming.

The girls of cabin 12 didn't know whether to run or stay and enjoy the show. They backed a little farther into the shadows but stayed to watch the scene play out.

A counselor soon emerged, saying, "Amberlie, be still or I can't help you."

"I can't be still! There's a giant snake, or a big spider, or something crawling in my hair! *Get it off!*"

The girls saw that Amberlie was truly terrified. They almost felt sorry for her.

Almost.

Later, after the Camp Club Girls had climbed into their own beds and switched off the lamp, Elizabeth said, "I feel kind of bad."

"Yeah, me, too," said McKenzie.

Silence filled the room. It was interrupted first by Bailey's giggles, then Kate's, and soon they were all lost in an uncontrollable combination of guilt and giggles.

●—●—●

Elizabeth was awakened early the next morning by Bailey, who was shaking her back and forth. "Beth! Pssssst! Beth, wake up!"

Elizabeth opened one eye. It was still dark outside. "This better be an emergency, Bales," she mumbled.

"It is, Beth! It's a big emergency!"

Elizabeth sat up groggily. "What is it?" she asked.

"The talent show is tonight! We have to practice. Now."

Elizabeth dropped back down and pulled the covers over her head again. "Go to sleep, Bailey," she grumbled.

"But we have to practice, and everyone else who is in the talent show will want to practice today, too. That means the piano and the stage will be taken all day long. If we don't go now, we may not get a chance later, Beth!"

Elizabeth moaned. Bailey had a point. But sleep was more important to her at that moment.

Unfortunately, winning was more important to Bailey,

and she wasn't giving up easily. "Beth, please? Pretty please, Beth? Don't you want to beat Amberlie?"

Reluctantly, Elizabeth sat up once again. "Okay. But you owe me," she mumbled.

The two girls dressed quickly, left a note to let the others know where they were headed, and were halfway to the dining hall when the trumpet began to warble reveille. They pushed open the doors to the quiet building without paying much attention to where they were going. As they entered, someone else was exiting. A very tall someone with muddy boots and a large cup of coffee. The two girls collided with the man, spilling coffee all over the boots and the freshly mopped floor.

"Oh, I'm sorry!" both girls cried out before they realized who they were speaking to.

Mr. Gerhardt pulled a handkerchief out of his pocket and knelt to clean up the mess. "You girls are up early. Do you always wander around in the dark?" he asked.

"Oh, no, sir," said Elizabeth. "We just need the piano to practice for tonight's talent show."

Mr. Gerhardt gave them each a long, steely look then turned back to refill his coffee.

"We only have a couple of days of camp left," Elizabeth told Bailey, who stared after the man.

"Yeah," Bailey said. "If we're going to solve this mystery,

we need to move!"

The girls were now wide-awake and scurried through the inner doors of the dining hall. Elizabeth sat at the piano and began warming up with some scales. Bailey sat next to her and sang, "Do, re, mi, fa, so, la, ti, do." When both girls were warmed up, Bailey took the stage and began smiling at the tables and chairs.

"What are you doing?" asked Elizabeth.

"I'm practicing my smile," Bailey replied, as if it were the most obvious thing in the world.

Elizabeth chuckled and began playing the song. They ran through it three times before a line formed outside. "We'd better go," she told Bailey. "Come on, we can hold a place for the others."

The two stepped outside and took their places at the end of the short line. Before long, the rest of the Camp Club Girls joined them. "I can't believe you two got up so early," mumbled Kate. "The rest of us overslept. Biscuit is still in the room. We didn't have time to take him to the golf course, so we'll have to do that after breakfast."

"Oh, and tell her about the socks," Sydney urged.

"Oh, yeah, the room is a wreck. Biscuit got into the socks again," Kate told them. "The alarm clock didn't go off, and we woke up to Biscuit slinging Alex's smelly sock onto my head."

"Hey!" Alex protested. "My socks aren't any smellier than yours!"

"He got into the socks again? Great. What is the deal with that dog and dirty socks?" Bailey groaned.

"We need a plan. Why don't we get our breakfast to go? Kate, you and Alex take Biscuit to the golf course, and the rest of us will clean up the room."

"No, let me go instead of Alex," urged Bailey. "Maybe I can practice a few strokes!"

The other girls laughed at their youngest roommate. "Bailey, I don't know where you get all that energy, but you should bottle it and sell it," said Elizabeth.

The girls followed the rest of the line into the dining hall.

●—●—●

Kate, Bailey, and Biscuit entered the empty golf course, and Biscuit immediately ran for the pile of golf clubs stacked on the office porch. He returned with his favorite club. The handle was marked up and down with his teeth marks.

He dropped it at Bailey's feet and looked at her longingly. "Ew, sorry boy. I have to practice, and I'm not gonna do it with your slobbery club. I think I'll get a fresh one," she told him with a pat on the head. She headed over to select her own club.

Kate picked up the chewed-up golf club and looked at it. "I've never known of a dog who likes golf." She laughed.

"My dad plays golf. If only I could convince him to let you be his caddy, you could come home with me." She threw the golf club, and Biscuit bounded after it.

Bailey was on her third stroke when the sound of a golf cart interrupted them. Biscuit, who seemed afraid of Mr. Gerhardt, slipped behind the clown attraction, tripping the wire and causing the loud, silly laughter the girls had grown used to. Kate and Bailey were relieved to see that Mr. Anzer was with Gerhardt.

"You girls sure spend a lot of time down here," said Mr. Anzer as he climbed out of the cart.

The girls laughed nervously. "Yeah, I wanna be the next Tiger Woods," Bailey told him.

The old man smiled. "Sounds great. Then the rest of us will be able to say, 'We knew her when. . .'"

Kate glanced nervously over her shoulder, looking for Biscuit. Since that first day at the golf course, the little dog disappeared every time Gerhardt came around. But he had drawn attention to himself with the clown's laughter. Gerhardt looked toward the clown then started walking that way.

"Is that the dog I ran off last week?" he asked. "I keep seeing his paw prints around, but I can never catch him. I've called the pound. They should be out sometime today or tomorrow."

Suddenly, Biscuit took off.

"Hey, mutt! Come back here!" yelled Gerhardt, chasing the little dog. Biscuit slipped through the gate, and he was gone. Gerhardt examined the gate then walked toward his office. "I'll fix this problem. That back gate is going to be fastened for good."

The color drained out of Kate's face, and she looked like she was going to be sick. Bailey gently touched her friend's arm and whispered, "It's okay. We'll find him. He'll probably find us first."

Kate gulped then nodded. She couldn't do anything about it now.

"You girls need to get to class, don't you? You'll be late," said Mr. Anzer.

The girls nodded then headed out the gate. When they were out of earshot, Kate said, "What will we do now? Gerhardt said the pound is coming. We've got to find Biscuit before they do, or he'll be lost to us forever!"

"Well, I'd rather the pound find him than that cougar! At least they won't hurt him," said Bailey. "Come on. If we hurry, we might be able to catch the others before class. Let's see if they have any ideas."

The two girls ran back to the cabin and arrived just as the others were leaving. "Biscuit!" Kate said, stopping to catch her breath.

The girls could read the pain in Kate's eyes. "What's wrong?" McKenzie asked.

"He's gone!" exclaimed Bailey. "And the pound is coming for him today!"

Kate and Bailey took turns explaining what had happened, and the others listened with concern.

"What can we do?" asked Kate in a worried voice.

"We'll divide up right now and search the woods," suggested Alex.

"We can't miss class. We'll get in trouble," said Elizabeth.

"I know what we'll do," offered Sydney. "Mac and I go on a nature walk with our class this morning. We'll walk right through the woods where Biscuit is hiding. Why don't we each carry a backpack filled with treats. . .something he'll smell. Maybe then he'll find us. If he does, we can slip him into the backpack."

The others agreed that this sounded like a good plan—at least until later when they could search more freely.

"What kind of treat should we put in your backpacks?" Bailey asked.

The girls offered suggestions, from stale cheese crackers to leftover biscuits. But Elizabeth offered the winning solution.

Minutes later, Sydney and McKenzie left the cabin, each with a backpack filled with dirty socks.

—•—

"Today is our last day to practice before the big contest," Miss Rebecca told her students. "I am very pleased with how much scripture you have memorized. As you know, memorizing God's Word is one of the most important things you can do. That's why the winner of this competition will receive double points for her team. So, who's ready to get started?"

Hands shot up around the room until the counselor called on Elizabeth. Then all hands went down. "Oh, come on, doesn't anybody want to compete with Elizabeth?" Miss Rebecca asked with a smile.

The class laughed. Elizabeth had a reputation for being a scriptural encyclopedia.

Finally, Amberlie raised her hand. "I'll do it, Miss Rebecca," she said sweetly.

"Wonderful! Come to the front. For this first part, I'll give the reference, and then you say the complete verse with the reference at the end. Every once in a while, I may stop and ask what the verse means. Ready?"

Both girls nodded.

"Elizabeth, you first. Proverbs 20:15."

Elizabeth smiled. " 'Gold there is, and rubies in abundance, but lips that speak knowledge are a rare jewel,' Proverbs 20:15."

Good job. Amberlie, Proverbs 3:13–14."

Amberlie smiled sweetly. "Certainly, Miss Rebecca. 'Blessed is the man who finds wisdom, the man who gains understanding, for she is more profitable than silver and yields better returns than gold,' Proverbs 3:13–14."

"Very good, Amberlie. I'm impressed! You've been holding out on us," said the counselor.

Amberlie beamed. But when Miss Rebecca turned to address the class, the girl leaned toward Elizabeth and whispered, "You're toast, Anderson."

Elizabeth smiled. "Bring it on," she whispered back.

●—●—●

The nature hike provided some interesting clues in the search for Biscuit, but the girls couldn't find the little dog. At one point, Sydney spotted paw prints in the mud, which looked the size of Biscuit's. But the girls couldn't disrupt class by calling out for the little dog, so they just kept hiking. They tried to mark the spot in their minds so they could come back and search later.

The girls gathered at the cabin for Discovery Time, and Elizabeth said a special prayer. "Dear Lord, please keep Biscuit safe! Please help us to find him before the pound does. And please help us to solve the mystery of Mr. Gerhardt's digging. Amen."

"Amen," the girls echoed.

"We have two goals for today," said Alex. "We have to

find Biscuit. And we have to find out why Mr. Gerhardt is digging at the golf course every night. We know he's probably looking for the missing jewels that were never found when his father was convicted."

McKenzie jumped in. "Perhaps we should stop concentrating on why he's digging, and start digging ourselves."

The rest of the girls looked at McKenzie. "You're brilliant!" exclaimed Sydney. "Why didn't we think of that before?"

The girls divided into two teams. Kate, Sydney, and Elizabeth would search for Biscuit, and the other three would search the golf course for hidden treasure.

Kate would take her cell phone into the woods, and the other three would carry Elizabeth's cell phone with them. That way they could maintain contact in case the jewels were found.

Or in case any cougars showed up.

●—●—●

When they arrived at the golf course, Alex, Sydney, and McKenzie heard Mr. Gerhardt's voice from inside the office building. Sneaking to the window, they listened to the man talking frantically. There were no other voices, so he must have been talking on the phone.

"I know, I know. The golf course is a mess. But I'm. . ."

He stopped to listen to the other person. Then he

started again. "I know. But trust me, I have a good reason for digging things up. I'll fix it before the next camp begins, I promise."

More silence.

"I can't tell you why."

Quiet.

"I know I can trust you, but. . ."

There was a long pause, and then Gerhardt sighed. "Okay. I'll tell you everything, but it will take awhile. I'll meet you in your office at two o'clock."

More silence.

Then he said, "Okay. I'll see you at the stables at two o'clock." They heard the man hang up. "Oh, dear God," he said, "if those jewels are here, please let me find them. Please help me prove my father's innocence."

The girls looked at one another, wide-eyed, then headed back toward the main camp. As soon as they were out of earshot, Sydney spoke. "It sounds like he's going to spill the beans to Mr. Anzer. We've got to figure out a way to listen in on that conversation!"

Golf Clubs and Socks

Alex, Sydney, and McKenzie were halfway back to the cabins when they remembered the cell phone. "Let's call and check on the others," McKenzie said.

Kate answered the phone right away. "Did you find the jewels?" she asked without saying "hello."

"No, but we may be very close to solving the mystery. How about you all? Any sign of Biscuit?" asked McKenzie.

"We saw signs of him but no Biscuit. Sydney led us to where you two found his paw prints this morning. We've called and called, but we can't find him. We're headed back now. We'll search some more after lunch." Kate sounded sad.

"Don't worry, we'll find him. Meet us back at the cabin. We have a lot to discuss," McKenzie told her.

All six girls were back at the cabin within ten minutes, discussing Gerhardt's phone conversation.

"How can we listen in on that conversation? The stables are busier than the golf course. We can't just stand by the window; that would look suspicious," said Elizabeth.

"I have an idea," said Kate. "Let me see Elizabeth's phone...."

— • —

After lunch, the girls headed to the stables. They had talked about splitting up again to search for Biscuit, but only Kate was willing to miss the conversation. And they agreed it wasn't safe for Kate to search the woods alone.

"We'll all go search as soon as we hear what Mr. Gerhardt says," Elizabeth promised.

The girls walked casually into the stable area, admiring the horses and talking about riding the trails. They each played their parts well.

"Hello, girls!" greeted Mr. Anzer. "What can I do for you today?"

"Well, um, I actually have a question," said Kate. "Could I talk to you in your office?"

The old man smiled. "Certainly, young lady." He held the door open for her then followed her inside. "What can I do for you?"

Kate took a deep breath then began talking. She fingered the telephone in her pocket, ready to press Elizabeth's number on the speed dial. "I live in the city—Philadelphia—but I'd really like to spend more time around animals. Are there any clubs I could join that would let me be around horses even though I don't have room for one at my house?"

"Why, certainly! I'm sure an equestrian organization is near you. I'll check into it and get back to you before you leave camp." Mr. Anzer smiled. "Was that all you wanted?"

Um, yes, sir. Thank you so much," she answered. As the gray-haired man stood, she pressed the button. She heard Elizabeth's phone ringing just outside the door. Suddenly, she heard Amberlie's voice.

"You think you're so smart, Elizabeth! But you just wait. I'm gonna smear you in that scripture memory competition, and every other competition. You and your little team will wish you never came to Camp Discovery Lake!"

Mr. Anzer was out the door in a moment, and Kate quickly slid her phone under a corner of his desk, then followed him out. Elizabeth's phone was still ringing.

"Amberlie, may I see you in my office, please?" Mr. Anzer said sternly.

Amberlie, clearly surprised, turned syrupy sweet. "Oh, hello, Mr. Anzer. Elizabeth and I were just. . ."

"I heard you, Amberlie. Now step into my office, please," he told her.

Her face held a mixture of defiance and fear as she stepped into the room. Elizabeth answered her phone just as Mr. Anzer shut the door.

The six girls didn't know what to do. They had meant to plant the phone for Gerhardt's conversation. Now they could hear Mr. Anzer's conversation with Amberlie. Sydney took the phone from Elizabeth, held her finger to her lips, and pressed the button for the speakerphone. Alex kept watch at the stable entry as the conversation was broadcast for them all to hear.

"Amberlie, I don't understand you," came Mr. Anzer's voice through the phone. "You're a smart, beautiful, talented girl. You act sweet around adults, but you don't have any of us fooled. You are mean and spiteful to the other girls your age. Why?"

"I don't know," Amberlie said softly.

There was a long silence. Then Mr. Anzer said, "You know, Amberlie, my father was a pastor. When I was a little boy, I felt like everyone expected me to be perfect. I wasn't allowed to act silly or get into mischief or make the normal mistakes that most kids made. I felt like I had to be perfect. Sometimes I envied the other kids because their lives seemed so. . .normal."

The girls heard sniffles. Then sobs. Finally, Amberlie spoke. "It's not fair! Those other girls get to do whatever they want, and nobody expects anything of them! Everyone expects me to be polite, to make good grades, to be clean and tidy. I feel like I'm being judged all the time by everyone."

Mr. Anzer said, "Here is a box of tissues. I know exactly how you feel. But you know what I finally learned?"

"What?" the girl asked.

"Most people weren't judging me at all. Oh, a few were. But most of them just loved me and wanted me to be happy."

Amberlie sniffled. "Really?" she asked.

The girls outside the door were silent. None felt right about eavesdropping on this conversation. But they needed to keep the phone on so they could hear Gerhardt. Finally, Elizabeth took the phone from Sydney and flipped it shut. "This is wrong," she said. "We'll just have to forget about Gerhardt. We don't need to eavesdrop. I feel almost like we're stealing something. . . ."

The other girls nodded.

"We were stealing a conversation that didn't belong to us," said McKenzie. The girls were just leaving when the office door opened again. No one looked at Amberlie as she walked past them.

Kate approached the office door as Mr. Anzer was leaving. "I left something in your office," she said and retrieved the phone. The girls left the stables in silence. They had a lot to think about.

The girls spent the next hour in the woods searching for Biscuit. But either the little dog had escaped to the other side of the woods, or else. . .well, they didn't want to think about the "or else."

Finally, tired and sweaty, they gave up. Bailey and Elizabeth decided to go back to the cabin to shower and prepare for the talent show. The others decided to snoop around the golf course and perhaps do some digging of their own.

When they arrived at the golf course, Sydney, McKenzie, and Alex started examining the piles of dirt. Kate sat on the office porch and looked at the pile of golf clubs. Biscuit's chewed-up club was on top of the pile, and she picked it up. She sat holding the club and thinking of her little lost dog when her phone rang. It was her father.

"Hello, Katy-kins! Are you still having fun at camp? Do you miss your ol' dad at all? I can't wait to see you tomorrow evening!" Her dad's voice was loving and familiar. The sound of it brought the tears that had threatened all day. Before she knew it, she was pouring out her heart.

"Daddy! I found a dog, and I named him Biscuit, and he has been my dog for the whole camp, and I taught him to sit and to stay, and he sleeps at my feet, and he's the best dog in the whole world, and. . .and. . .he's gone!"

"Whoa, there! Slow down! Why don't you back up and

tell me what you're talking about," her father told her.

She sat on the porch, holding the tooth-marked golf club and telling her daddy the whole story of Biscuit. When she finished, he remained quiet.

Finally, he said, "You say he's been sleeping with you in your bed?"

"Yes, sir," she answered.

"And he's not bitten or hurt you or the other girls?"

"Oh, no, sir! He's the sweetest, gentlest, smartest dog in the world!" she told him.

"Well, your mother and I have talked about letting you have a dog. I'll call the camp director. If they find him, as long as he is healthy, you can keep him," her father told her.

"Really? You mean it?" Kate asked, hardly believing her ears.

As Kate hung up the phone, her spirits were lifted, but only for a moment. Right now, she had no idea where Biscuit was. She didn't know if she'd ever see him again. She picked up the golf club, walked to the fence, and tossed it into the woods. If Biscuit came back, maybe he'd find the club and bring it to her, wanting to play fetch.

●—●—●

The crowd was growing, and Bailey was getting nervous. She stood with Elizabeth behind the curtain, watching the chairs fill. "We just have to win, Elizabeth! We just have to! This could be my big break, you know?"

Elizabeth smiled at her friend, who looked ridiculous in her pink curlers and face cream. "You'll be great, Bales. Just relax. If you don't make it to Hollywood, you always have golfing to fall back on."

"Yeah," said Bailey. "Too bad there wasn't more interest in the golf course. I would have won a golfing competition for sure."

Soon, the camp director was on stage testing the microphones. When she was certain all was working properly, she began her speech. "Good evening, ladies. As you know, Camp Discovery Lake is almost over. Tonight's talent competition marks the beginning of the final competitions, which will continue all day tomorrow.

Before we begin, I want to tell you how proud I am and how proud all the counselors are of all of you. You have been a wonderful group of ladies, and I believe you have experienced real growth here during the last two weeks. You've learned about all sorts of things, but the most important thing we've tried to teach you is that nothing is more important than your relationship with God."

The woman continued with a reminder about being supportive and polite to all the contestants, and before long, the first act was introduced.

Elizabeth and Bailey were third on the program, just after a baton twirler and before a tap-dancing duet. When their act was introduced, they were surprised by loud cheers and applause. The Camp Club Girls had a reputation for being friendly to everyone, and it was paying off.

Elizabeth began playing, and Bailey performed. The audience laughed in all the right places. When she finished, she bowed, and the room erupted in more applause. Then she gestured toward Elizabeth, who also bowed, and the girls left the stage.

They were nearly knocked over by their four roommates. "You were awesome! Bailey, you're a natural! And Elizabeth, you can really play! We'll win this for sure!"

The group was hushed by a counselor as the next act was introduced. The girls sat and politely applauded when the dance number was finished. The next act was Amberlie, and the girls held their breaths. They had a feeling she would be their main competition.

Amberlie took the stage and held the microphone. The music began, and the girl began to sing. Her voice was pure and sweet, and she sang a popular Christian song almost better than the original artist. The audience leaned forward, drinking in her voice.

Then, at a climactic point in the song, a dreadful howling noise sounded from outside the window. It got louder and louder, and more and more dreadful. At first the audience thought Amberlie had really messed up. But the Camp Club Girls knew that howl. Without thinking, Kate jumped to her feet and ran out the door, yelling, "Biscuit! You're okay!"

Her five roommates followed, creating quite a stir in the room. Amberlie, who had just sounded like an angel from heaven, stopped the song. "I can't believe this!" she yelled. "Those girls did this on purpose so they would win! This isn't fair!" She slammed her microphone into its stand and stormed off the stage.

The girls exited the dining hall just in time to see two men getting out of a large white van. It had the words ANIMAL CONTROL painted on the side. Gerhardt spoke to the men, one with a long stick and the other with a net.

"Oh, no! What will we do now?" whispered Kate. The howling continued as campers and counselors poured out of the building.

Elizabeth thought quickly. "Kate, you and Sydney come with me. Alex, Bailey, and McKenzie, create a distraction."

"A distraction?" questioned McKenzie.

Alex grabbed her with one hand, Bailey with the other, and said, "Come with me!" She led them to the men beside the white truck. "Excuse me?" she interrupted.

The men looked at the girls, their eyes resting on Bailey

and her silly costume.

"That howling has interrupted our talent show. What kind of animal is that?" Alex asked.

"We believe it's a dog, miss. Now if you'll. . ."

"You have such a dangerous job. It must be scary to have to catch these animals. I mean, you don't know if they have rabies or if they will attack you. Have you ever been bitten?" she continued.

As the men looked at Alex with annoyance and confusion, Kate, Elizabeth, and Sydney moved toward the howls. Biscuit seemed to be in the woods across from the dining hall. As they moved into the shadows, Kate flipped open her cell phone for light.

"Biscuit!" they called. The howls were getting closer, but they couldn't find the little dog.

"He must be stuck," said Sydney, "or he would have come to us by now."

The girls continued the search but soon heard men's voices behind them. A large spotlight shined on them, and Mr. Gerhardt called out, "You girls get back to the dining hall. You could get hurt out here!"

Suddenly, they heard one of the men yell, "I found him! He's stuck in this hole. Poor little guy! Good thing he didn't get stuck out here a few days ago, before we hauled off that cougar. He would have eaten this little fellow for lunch!"

The man walked into the spotlight holding a very wiggly, very dirty Biscuit in his arms. When Biscuit saw Kate, he lunged out of the man's grip and ran for his beloved owner.

But Gerhardt was too quick for the dog. He stepped in front of Kate, saying, "Oh, no you don't. You're not getting away again!"

Biscuit changed directions and dashed toward the dining hall. Campers and counselors squealed as the filthy dog ran into the building, followed by three men and six girls, all yelling, "Come back!"

The man with the net cornered the dog on the stage, but just as the net was coming down on him, Biscuit took off again and headed back out the door. The big man leaped for the dog and crashed into a row of chairs.

Out the door came the little dog, then Gerhardt, then Kate and Sydney, then the man with the pole, then Bailey with her curlers and face cream, then the other three Camp Club Girls. The man with the net followed, limping.

Biscuit led the group toward the golf course. The men gradually slowed, holding their sides and breathing heavily. The girls raced ahead, and as they reached the fence, they found Biscuit, tail wagging, with his favorite golf club in his mouth.

"Biscuit!" Kate yelled, and scooped the filthy dog into

her arms. "I'm so glad you're safe!"

The dog clung to the golf club, and the girls laughed. "Bailey, I know you want to be the next Tiger Woods, but I think Biscuit may give you a run for your money," said Elizabeth.

Just then, Mr. Anzer's golf cart pulled up. Gerhardt sat beside him, and the two Animal Control men were in the backseat. Several of the counselors followed, including Miss Rebecca. Gerhardt jumped out of the cart and stepped toward Kate. "You need to put the dog down," he said sternly. He grabbed the golf club, but Biscuit growled and refused to let go.

The tug-of-war continued, Kate holding Biscuit, Biscuit holding one end of the golf club, and Mr. Gerhardt pulling on the other end of the club.

Suddenly, the club broke apart, and out spilled an old sock.

Everyone gasped as the contents of the sock tumbled out!

Real Treasure

No one moved. They stood in the moonlight, with the golf cart headlights casting a soft glow on the broken golf club, the old sock, and the sparkly, shiny jewels that had fallen from it.

Then Mr. Gerhardt sank to his knees. Tears trickled down his cheeks as he gathered the colorful treasures. "Thank you, God! We found them!"

The girls jumped up and down and cheered, and the man looked confused. Elizabeth stepped forward. "We know all about your father, Mr. Gerhardt. We know he was convicted of stealing these jewels and selling them on the black market. And we know he didn't do it."

The man stood up. "But. . .but how did you—"

Alex spoke up. "We were curious about your digging. We figured that the spooky sounds weren't real, and we figured you were behind them. So we decided to do a little investigating of our own."

"When Mr. Anzer told me about the thieves that used

to hide in that old house, we put two and two together. You looked pretty suspicious for a while," Elizabeth told the man.

The adults who had followed them to the golf course were now gathered around, listening intently.

"We went to the house, as you know. There we found an old newspaper with an article about the stolen jewels. I did an Internet search and found out your father was convicted for stealing them," said Kate.

"Yeah," Sydney interjected. "But we also learned that the jury was divided. That there wasn't real proof of his guilt."

"It didn't make sense," McKenzie added her two cents. "If your father was guilty, he would have just told you where the jewels were hidden. You wouldn't have been digging those holes everywhere!"

"That's when we decided the thieves must have hidden them somewhere at the golf course. We searched but didn't find anything. And just think, all this time, Biscuit was trying to give us the answer!" Elizabeth concluded.

Gerhardt nodded. "I've been trying to prove my father's innocence for nearly twenty years. I've searched high and low, but the jewels were just gone. Then, several months ago, I found out the thieves had hidden in that old house, and I had a feeling this was my big break. I searched the area, and the golf course seemed the most logical hiding place for the jewels. After all, who would think to look at a kids' camp?

"That's why I really didn't want you girls snooping around. I was afraid you'd find them first and not tell anyone about them. I didn't mean to scare you girls." His eyes fell on Bailey. "I'm sorry I frightened you so much. I hope you'll forgive me," he said.

Bailey's cold-creamed face shone in the moonlight, and she smiled her million-dollar smile. "You're forgiven. Besides, this has been the most exciting two weeks of my life!"

The man tousled her hair then looked at Biscuit. "And you, little dog, are a hero. Just think, I've been trying to get rid of you, and you ended up finding the jewels for me!" He patted the filthy dog on the head, and Biscuit let out a friendly bark.

Kate laughed. "He has a thing for smelly old socks. That explains why he was so drawn to this golf club! All this time we were trying to solve the mystery at Discovery Lake, and Biscuit had the answer the whole time!"

Mr. Anzer approached Kate, examining the dog in her arms. "So this is the little guy who caused such a stir around here. He is quite the mystery maker, leaving evidence of his presence all over camp. But we could never find him! Now we know why. You were hiding him!"

Kate smiled sheepishly.

"I spoke with your father on the phone this evening, Kate," he continued. "I called him to discuss an equestrian society I located in Philadelphia, and he wanted to talk about dogs!" The group laughed, and Mr. Anzer reached for Biscuit. "You can keep this little fellow, but tonight he needs to go with the Animal Control men. They'll make sure he is healthy and is caught up on his shots. They'll probably even give him a bath before they bring him back to you!"

"Good luck with that!" said Sydney, and all the girls laughed.

Miss Rebecca stepped forward. "This explains the strange smells from your room. I just thought you girls were really stinky," she said with a wink. "And the socks! He must be the one who kept your room in a mess!" She knelt down, and Biscuit licked her on the nose.

The Camp Club Girls told Biscuit good-bye, and Kate held him tightly before handing him to Mr. Anzer. "I'm so glad you're safe, Biscuit. You really had me worried! After tomorrow, we'll never have to be apart again!"

Biscuit wagged his tail and covered her face with sloppy kisses before being carried to the Animal Control men. The limping man took him gently and slid into Mr.

Anzer's cart. "Would you mind giving us a lift?" he asked the old gentleman.

The group of girls and counselors followed the golf cart back to the dining hall, and the talent show was soon back under way.

● — ● — ●

The girls awakened early the next morning, listening to the annoying trumpet reveille for the last time. They stretched and groaned. Bailey clutched her oversized panda under one arm and her blue ribbon in the other hand. She had been thrilled to win first prize in the talent show and had fallen asleep with the ribbon under her pillow.

"Okay, girls. Today is the day we win or lose," said Sydney. "Even with Bailey's points, we're still behind. Biscuit made sure we didn't win the cleanest cabin award. We have to win almost all of the competitions today, or we won't walk away as champions."

"We'll win. We have to win. We're the Camp Club Girls," said McKenzie.

Alex bounced to the center of the room. "Remind me again who is doing which competition?"

Kate sat up in her bed. "I took the nature studies quiz yesterday, and we'll find out our scores today at breakfast."

"I'm competing in scripture memory," said Elizabeth. "Mac, aren't you doing the horse-riding competition?"

"Yes," McKenzie replied. "I signed up yesterday."

"Alex, will you compete with me in the canoe races?" Sydney asked. "I really want to do that, but I need a partner."

"That sounds like fun. I think we really have a chance to win!" Alex said.

A short time later, as the girls sat at their usual breakfast table, the camp director took the microphone. "Good morning, ladies. May I have your attention?"

Miss Barr continued. "I hope you're ready for an exciting, fun-filled last day of camp. As you know, the Camp Club Girls of cabin 12 took the winning points last night at our talent competition." She paused for applause. "But the Princess Pack from cabin 8 is still in the lead. They had the cleanest cabin almost every day!" She paused again, but not as many people clapped.

"I have just received the results from the nature studies quiz taken yesterday," the woman continued. "Believe it or not, we have a three-way tie! Equal points will be given to Grace Collins of the Princess Pack, Rachel Smith of the Shooting Starlets, and Kate Oliver of the Camp Club Girls. Congratulations to each of you and your teams!"

The room erupted into a combination of applause and disappointed groans. "The first competition this morning will be barrel racing. The races begin at nine a.m., so I suggest you all finish your breakfast and head that way."

The woman replaced the microphone into the stand and stepped down from the stage.

The Camp Club Girls congratulated Kate, who seemed unaffected by her win. She simply smiled, thanked them, and continued devouring her bacon-filled biscuit.

The girls finished their breakfast and headed toward the stables. "Are you nervous?" Elizabeth asked McKenzie.

"Not really," Mac replied. "I love to ride. I just hope I get the horse I want."

"We'll cheer for you!" called Sydney as McKenzie headed for the corral.

She was relieved when she saw that Spirit didn't yet have a rider. She walked over to his stall and began saddling him.

"I've seen you ride. You're good," came a voice from the next stall. McKenzie was surprised to see it was Taylor, one of Amberlie's roommates.

"Thank you," she responded.

"Well, good luck out there," the girl called as she rode into the paddock.

McKenzie stared after the girl. She had assumed that all of Amberlie's friends were just as mean as Amberlie. But this girl had been. . .friendly. "I guess that will teach me to make snap judgments," she told Spirit.

The dozen girls that competed in barrel racing lined

up their horses. Most of them did a good job, but few had McKenzie's expertise. The Camp Club Girls' cheers could be heard above all others as they watched their friend effortlessly guide Spirit around the barrels and to the finish line, taking nearly a minute less than anyone else.

Mac smiled proudly, and her blush was almost darker than her auburn hair as she accepted the blue ribbon.

●—●—●

Elizabeth held a little white index card, reading the verse over and over. The other girls were confident that Elizabeth would win, but she wasn't so sure. Philippians 2:3–4 always tripped her up: "Do nothing out of selfish ambition or vain conceit, but in humility consider others better than yourselves. Each of you should look not only to your own interests, but also to the interests of others."

She always messed up on the "selfish ambition or vain conceit" part. She could never get those phrases in the right order. Taking a deep breath, she offered a silent prayer.

Miss Rebecca took the stage. "Welcome to the scripture memory competition. Round one will begin with verses you all have learned here at camp. I will give the reference for the verse. Then contestants must recite the complete passage word for word and repeat the reference. Any questions?"

No one spoke, and the two dozen contestants formed

wo lines on the stage.

"This will take awhile," whispered Kate, settling in her hair. But the contestants dropped like flies, and by round our, only three girls were left. Elizabeth stood at one end f the line and Amberlie at the other, with a quiet girl amed Caitlyn in the middle.

Miss Rebecca began the round with Elizabeth. "Phippians 2:3–4," she said.

Elizabeth took a deep breath and briefly closed her eyes n concentration. Her five roommates held their breath as heir friend began to speak.

"Come on, Beth, you can do it," whispered Bailey.

Elizabeth spoke. "Do nothing. . .out of. . .selfish conceit r vain ambition, but in humility consider others better. . ." he stopped and looked directly at Miss Rebecca. "That vasn't right, was it?" she asked.

The counselor shook her head but smiled. "No, I'm orry, Elizabeth. But you aren't disqualified yet. Remain on age until another contestant correctly says the verse."

Caitlyn began to recite the verse but messed up in the niddle. The audience leaned forward as Amberlie took the nicrophone. She smiled the sweet smile that was reserved or public use and began the verse. Without missing a eat, she recited it perfectly, and her team cheered.

Miss Rebecca said, "Congratulations to each of our

contestants. We are proud of all of you, and I hope yo
will continue to memorize God's Word. And a speci
congratulation goes to Amberlie and the Princess Pack fc
winning this competition."

The audience applauded politely and dispersed for th
next competition.

●—■—●

Sydney and Alex stood on the bank of the pond, lookin
fiercely competitive. They had to win this race if they ha
any hope of winning the championship.

"When the whistle blows, you will climb into you
boats, paddle to the marker in the center of the pond, the
turn around and canoe back," the counselor instructe(
"At no time during the race can you exit the boat. If yo
fall or jump out of the boat, you'll be disqualified. Pleas
make sure your life jackets are securely fastened."

Sydney and Alex checked each other's life jackets. "
think we can win," whispered Alex.

"We have to win," Sydney responded.

"On your marks. . .get set," the counselor called, the
blew the whistle.

The two Camp Club Girls launched their canoe wit
skill and speed, and easily floated into first place. "One–
two, one—two," shouted Sydney. They had spent mor
than a half hour after breakfast, sitting on dry groun(

practicing their timing and technique. Both girls were naturally athletic, and the strokes came easily. In no time, they reached the marker in the center of the lake and rowed around it.

Elizabeth, Kate, McKenzie, and Bailey stood on shore, cheering as loudly as they could. The two girls in the center of the pond paid no attention, however. They concentrated on paddling as fast as they could. When they were within yards of the finish line, Sydney turned around to give Alex a high five. "We did it!" she called out.

Alex, caught off guard, was thrown off balance. She leaned to one side, trying to regain control, but it was too late. The boat tipped.

Splash! Two girls fell ungracefully into the water only inches from the finish line.

Sydney stood and yelled, "No! No way! This cannot be happening!" just as two girls from another cabin sailed past them to win the race.

Alex sputtered and pushed hair out of her eyes. The four remaining Camp Club Girls stood in shock until McKenzie broke into laughter.

"That was the funniest thing I've ever seen!" she called out. "That moment made losing the race worth it!"

Sydney and Alex frowned at her. But then they looked at themselves and their overturned boat, mere inches from the finish line, and the humor of the situation began to sink in. They had to laugh.

"Here, let me give you a hand," said McKenzie, holding out her arm. Alex and Sydney both reached out, grabbed their auburn-haired friend, and pulled her into the water with them. "Hey!" McKenzie yelled.

"Now that," Sydney said with laughter, "was the funniest thing I have ever seen!"

•—•—•

Elizabeth watched out the window as buses lined up to transport girls to the airport. The Camp Club Girls sat near the back of the room, frantically jotting down phone numbers and e-mail addresses. Kate cuddled Biscuit, who had been returned to her just moments before.

The camp director, Miss Barr, took the stage, and the noise died down.

"Saying good-bye is always the most difficult part of the camp experience. I know you all have developed some lasting friendships during the last two weeks. I hope each of you will return next year. And now, let's announce this year's Discovery Lake champions. As you know, teams have built points during the entire camp. But the greatest source of points comes from the counselors' award, which is given to the team that has shown loyalty, friendship, and humility throughout the camp. This year, one special group of ladies has exhibited these characteristics in an outstanding way. Camp Club Girls, would you join me on stage?"

The girls looked at each other in shock and rose from their chairs. When they arrived on stage, Mr. Anzer and Mr. Gerhardt joined them.

"These girls have been friendly, sweet, and supportive during the past two weeks. But they have also gone above and beyond what anyone could expect of our campers," said Mr. Anzer.

Mr. Gerhardt took the microphone. "Girls, you helped me solve the mystery at Discovery Lake, and because of it, my father's name will be cleared, and he'll be set free. I'm pleased to award the Camp Club Girls with the title Team Discovery Lake. You deserve it!"

The room erupted in cheers. Elizabeth looked at the audience, and even Amberlie was clapping. Biscuit wiggled in Kate's arms, and the girls gathered into a group hug.

"We did it!" they called out, whooping and hollering.

"I wonder what mystery we'll solve next," Elizabeth said with a smile. Just then, her cell phone rang. It was her father, and she stepped away from the cheering group so she could hear.

"How's my girl?" asked her dad, and she filled him in on their win. "That's great," he told her. "I have a surprise for you. When you get home, you won't even need to unpack your bags!"

"What do you mean?" she asked him.

"We're going to Washington, D.C.! We leave on Monday."

Elizabeth had always wanted to visit the capital, and now she had a friend there. After hanging up the phone, she went to find Sydney.

As the girls said their final good-byes and promised to keep in touch, they had no idea that another mystery was already beckoning the Camp Club Girls. From their various corners of the United States, soon they'd be embroiled in *Sydney's D.C. Discovery*.

"It was great to find the jewels for Mr. Gerhardt," Elizabeth commented as the girls hugged each other. "But the real treasure I found. . ." Elizabeth paused as she looked, in turn, into the faces of Kate, Bailey, Sydney, McKenzie, and Alex. "The real treasure is finding friends like you!"

If you enjoyed

MYSTERY AT DISCOVERY LAKE

be sure to read other

CAMP CLUB GIRLS

books from BARBOUR PUBLISHING

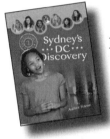

Book 2: Sydney's DC Discovery
ISBN 978-1-60260-268-7

Book 3: McKenzie's Montana Mystery
ISBN 978-1-60260-269-4

Book 4: Alexis and the Sacramento Surprise
ISBN 978-1-60260-270-0

Book 5: Kate's Philadelphia Frenzy
ISBN 978-1-60260-271-7

Book 6: Bailey's Peoria Problem
ISBN 978-1-60260-272-4